FIRE POWER

"Do it, Canyon!" Hirum Merchant said. "It's our only chance against five rifles."

Canyon O'Grady squatted behind Hirum's invention and squeezed the trigger. Before he could get his finger off the metal, six rounds burst forth. Two horses went down. One man was blown out of the saddle.

Canyon fired another burst. He saw the rounds blast into a horse's head and the man behind it. The rider took three rounds in the chest and two in his face. He cartwheeled to the ground and sprawled in the Missouri mud.

"I . . . I had no idea how deadly it could be," Hirum gasped.

Canyon could only shake his head. "Mr. Merchant . . . this weapon is awesome . . . it's hell-fire. . . ."

MACHINE GUN MADNESS

by
Jon Sharpe

A SIGNET BOOK

NEW AMERICAN LIBRARY

A DIVISION OF PENGUIN BOOKS USA INC.

NAL BOOKS ARE AVAILABLE AT QUANTITY DISCOUNTS WHEN USED TO
PROMOTE PRODUCTS OR SERVICES. FOR INFORMATION PLEASE WRITE
TO PREMIUM MARKETING DIVISION, NEW AMERICAN LIBRARY, 1633
BROADWAY, NEW YORK, NEW YORK 10019.

SIGNET TRADEMARK REG. U.S. PAT OFF. AND FOREIGN COUNTRIES
REGISTERED TRADEMARK—MARCA REGISTRADA
HECHO EN CHICAGO, U.S.A.

SIGNET, SIGNET CLASSIC, MENTOR, ONYX, PLUME,
MERIDIAN and NAL BOOKS are published by New American
Library, a division of Penguin Books USA Inc., 1633 Broadway,
New York, New York 10019

First Printing, September, 1989

1 2 3 4 5 6 7 8 9

PRINTED IN THE UNITED STATES OF AMERICA

Canyon O'Grady

His was a heritage of blackguards and poets, fighters and lovers, men who could draw a pistol and bed a lass with the same ease.

Freedom was a cry seared into Canyon O'Grady, justice a banner of the heart.

With the great wave of those who fled to America, the new land of hope and heartbreak, solace and savagery, he came to ride the untamed wildness of the Old West.

With a smile or a six-gun, Canyon O'Grady became a name feared by some and welcomed by others but remembered by all . . .

Short Creek, Missouri, eighty miles south of Kansas City near the Kansas border, on July 14, 1860. The trek to find Hirum Merchant and his amazing new gun that fired six hundred rounds a minute . . .

1

Ten Osage warriors had been circling the small frame house and yi-yipping just out of pistol range for a half-hour. All of the warriors were mounted on war ponies, all had bows and arrows, and one carried an old flintlock rifle he might not know how to fire. They darted in toward the door yelling and screaming, then slanted away, guiding their horses with only their knees.

Now one raced forward on his war pony and sent an arrow smashing through the kitchen window.

Soon all of them shot arrows into the windows of the small house. One of the braves paused at the side to blow a coal into a flame, then he lit a torch and raced toward the house.

Jolting through the yells and calls of the Osage came the snarling report of a heavy rifle. The warrior with the burning torch and a row of eagle feathers on his browband slammed off his war pony, a chunk of lead through his heart and lodged near his backbone. He sprawled in the Missouri dust never to move again.

Before the Indians realized they were under attack, a second report sounded and another Osage took a bullet high in the shoulder, sending him half off his pony. The warrior clung to the horse's mane, slumping forward as he raced off toward a creek a quarter of a mile away.

In a clump of brush two hundred yards from the house, a man lay, his eye pressed to the sight of a Spencer carbine. He tracked another Osage and fired. The attacking Indian took the round in his chest, screamed, and fell off his war pony.

Now the Indians looked in his direction, attracted by the pall of blue smoke the three shots had left just at the edge of the brush.

Four of the Osage turned and screeched at one another, then charged his position. The big man with a shock of flame-red hair who lay in the brush rolled toward a big cottonwood tree trunk and came to a kneeling position. He worked the trigger guard of the Spencer quickly, blasting lead at the charging Indians.

He knocked two of them off their horses before they were within fifty yards of him. They wheeled and headed back as he fired the last of the eight shots from the Spencer. He had drawn his big army percussion Colt revolver, but when he saw them wheel away, he upended the Spencer and quickly pulled out the empty tube from the butt of the weapon and pushed in a new tube filled with seven new rounds.

He chambered one and then sent six more shots at the Osage, who now streaked away, using the small house as cover against his rifle fire. When he was sure they were gone, the tall man rose and walked cautiously into the open, where he bent and checked the first of the fallen Indians. Two were dead. He had just bent over the third when a woman's voice cried out a warning.

He swung around, the Colt coming with him, and he fired automatically at one of the wounded Indians who had lifted up and started to throw a knife at him. The slug took the Osage in the left eye and drove him back into the dirt.

Canyon O'Grady checked the last two bodies, determined that they were dead, and looked up at the girl standing in the back door of the small house. First he saw the blue dress, nipped in at the waist and flaring at the breasts, buttoned protectively to wrist and chin.

Then he saw a billowing mass of long blond hair

cascading around her shoulders and down her back. The six-gun she held seemed out of place, and he noted that wisps of gunsmoke still came from the muzzle. Her pale-green eyes looked up at him as he walked forward. She saw a strapping man well over six feet, a shock of red hair and crackling blue eyes in a roguish face. She seemed to beat back tears as she smiled. "You saved my life. I thank you."

"Aye, lass. Osage, I'd say." There was a lilt of Ireland in his voice.

"Yes, they come through here now and then. Usually a shot or two near them and they move on."

"These were unusual, then."

She held the six-gun in front of her, not pointing it at him, but ready to. "You just passing by?"

"Might be. Looking for Hirum Merchant. In town they told me he lived here."

"Sometimes. He's gone right now. What would you want with him?"

"Business. Hear he's a gunsmith."

The girl nodded, her eyes a bit wary, blond hair rustling like ready-to-cut wheat. Now he saw that her nose was finely made, soft blond eyebrows, and a mouth that was set now in a firm pink line. A dimple would dent one cheek if she smiled, he was sure.

"Yes, Pa's an excellent gunsmith, but he doesn't hire out right now."

"Still and all, I need to see him."

"Likes of you is why he left two months ago. So many people came to see him he couldn't get his work done."

"That work he's doing is why I need to see him. I'd say I did you a favor, lass, with those Osage. Where I come from people are proud to repay favors. I think it's time for you to return the favor to me. The Osage were about to burn you right out of that house. I'd imagine you know what they'd do to the likes of a beautiful girl like you once you were out of rounds for that revolver of yours."

"I know what they would do." She sighed and lifted her glance to lock with his. The revolver swung down and she pointed it at the ground. "I'm truly grateful for your help. I was so frightened I could hardly shoot. First I liked it out here away from the rest of town, but today I didn't."

"I still need to find your father," he pressed.

He could see the emotions sweeping through her: gratitude to him, loyalty to her father. At last she sighed once more. "You come inside and I'll sit you down to some coffee and we'll talk some."

The house was neat, no dirty dishes on the ledge at the side of the kitchen. She took out a clean coffeepot and made a quick, fast-burning fire in a small cast-iron stove.

"Coffee be ready soon. I still can't tell you where Pa went. He made me promise. Said it was important that he get done with his work."

Canyon sat down in the offered chair and watched the sleek young woman getting the coffee started. When she turned, the movement brought the swell of her full breasts tight against the gingham dress. He watched in open admiration.

"The importance of your pa's work is why I'm here, Miss Merchant. My name is Canyon O'Grady, and I want to help your father get his work done."

"If you're looking to buy it, he isn't ready to sell."

"I don't want to buy it, lass."

"At least I know you're full of Irish blarney. I'm sorry, I can't help you."

Canyon looked out the window. "Time was when a person would be grateful for even the smallest favor. Now someone gets her life saved and it's good for only a fine thank-you and a beautiful smile."

"Pa said he was working on something important."

"That he is. The United States Army and the President of the United States are both highly interested in Hirum Merchant's new rapid-firing gun. We know a little about it. We have also heard that others are trying to steal it from him.''

"The President of the United States?" She looked up at him with awe, then suspicion. "The president? I really don't know whether to believe that or not.''

"You should. You probably haven't heard that there are a lot of people right now interested in making a gun like your father is working on. There are men from our own country who have said that they will find your father, steal his gun, and perhaps take him with them and set up shop to finish the gun and then begin to manufacture them. These men are well known for their crooked dealings and will stop at nothing to get what they want. The president sent me to find your father and protect him.''

The girl sat down slowly. "You really mean it, don't you?" Her eyes went wide and she held out her hand. "Pleased to meet you, Canyon O'Grady. I'm Elizabeth Merchant." She continued to stare at him "You actually talked to President Buchanan?''

"Yes, six or seven times. I work for him. That's why I'm here. We think your father needs some protection. We have information that at least one foreign nation, as well as this band of Americans, is out to get your father's invention away from him by any means possible.''

"Oh, they can't do that. Pa has worked on this new gun for over two years now. We've almost starved at times. Then he'd have to take work as a gunsmith at some town. But every night—" Elizabeth stopped. "Oh, dear. I wonder if he's safe where he went? He didn't know somebody might actually try to steal the gun.''

"Someone could do far worse than that to your father, Miss Merchant.''

The pretty young woman frowned for a moment, then stood and paced up and down in the small kitchen. She looked at Canyon two or three times and finally stopped. "Say Pa is in danger and there are these men trying to find and hurt him, how do I know that you're not just another one of them?"

"You have only my word on that, Miss Merchant. And my open, honest Irish face."

"You don't have any kind of badge or a paper, or anything? Even a U.S. marshal has papers."

He took a folded paper from his wallet. It was signed by President Buchanan and said Canyon O'Grady was a United States agent. Everyone was urged to give him complete cooperation.

She read the paper and gave it back to him, then went to the cupboard and took out a dish of ham and beans and put it in a pot she placed on the iron stove. Then she added two sticks to the fire. She poured the coffee and watched Canyon.

"I'm not sure I trust you, Canyon O'Grady. Irishmen are not my favorite people."

Canyon grinned broadly. "You're sounding a little Irish yourself. Samuel Johnson said, 'The Irish are a fair people, they never speak well of one another.' But then, you know that Sam Johnson was an Englishman, so what can you expect?"

"Not saying I will, but if I was to be convinced I should take you to my pa, would you let me keep my six-gun?"

"Yes, I would. Two of them and a derringer and a knife if you want to carry them. But you don't have to take me anywhere. You can stay right here. Just tell me where he went so I can get to him as quickly as possible."

"No, I won't tell you a thing. If I decide to, I'll take you there and watch you closely. There's too much blarney in you for my way of thinking." She stared at him a minute, then shrugged. "Near sundown now. If you split me some wood, I can finish warming us some supper. Tomorrow morning I'll decide what I'm going to do."

"Where's the woodpile?"

A half-hour later Canyon came in with an armload of wood and stacked it neatly in the woodbox. The supper was simple but adequate and the coffee hot.

When the dishes were put away, she pointed at the door. "Canyon O'Grady, take your Irish wit and your bedroll and find a spot to sleep in the woods. I'll be inside with the door bolted and broken windows covered—and my six-gun under my pillow. I'll decide tomorrow."

"All right," Canyon agreed. "But I'll be ready to go tomorrow. I know you'll want the two of us to find your pa and warn him about the danger he's in."

He watched her a moment and saw her working on the big problem. Then he said good night, went out the door, and waited until he heard the bolt slam home. Canyon found a spot in the brush where he had fired at the Indians. He wanted to give the redskins plenty of room to return and pick up their dead as soon as it was dark. He was surprised they hadn't done so already. They would float in during darkness like ghost dancers retrieving their slain friends and would be no threat. The Osage, like most Indians, do not like to fight at night.

Canyon stretched out on his bedroll. The girl was worried about her father. He figured that she would decide, come morning, to go find him and would take Canyon along. There was really no other decision she could make.

Before he fell to sleep, Canyon went over his assignment again as he had been briefed by Major General Silas Warrenton. Many times President Buchanan himself gave Canyon his orders, but this problem was too urgent and there was no time for Canyon to go to Washington.

Canyon had been in St. Louis finishing up a case and had kept General Warrenton informed. He received a telegram a few days ago telling him to remain in place, a courier would be coming to hand-deliver a first-class secret document.

The courier met Canyon at his hotel, the Mid Western, had him write his name on a card, and compared it with a sample he brought with him. Then the courier took out a photograph and studied it against the real thing. When he was convinced that Canyon was who he said he was, he had him sign a receipt for the goods and went down to catch the next train back to Washington.

Canyon went up to his third-floor room and unsealed the envelope and began to read.

To: Canyon O'Grady, United States Agent.

From: Silas Warrenton, Major General USA, Military Aide to President Buchanan.

At once proceed to Kansas City, Missouri, and then south to a small town called Short Creek, and contact a gunsmith named Hirum Merchant.

Our information is that he is in the final stages of development of a new kind of rapid-firing gun that, if successful, will be a major leap forward in weaponry.

The United States government is interested in protecting Mr. Merchant from any outside influence, and wants to be sure that he has both the time and facilities to finish work on his weapon.

When you contact Mr. Merchant, explain to him the president's concern and urge him to be the guest of the government at the nearest United States military post or fort, where he will be given space and equipment and board and room as he works on his project.

Problems: We are not sure that Mr. Merchant is at the above given town. He may have left. He has a daughter who may or may not be with him. Your first job is to find the man. Your second task is to protect him from all those who would try to buy, steal, or destroy his new weapon, and to safeguard Merchant himself.

Second problem is that there is at least one foreign power now in Missouri, with several agents, determined to capture Mr. Merchant and steal his ideas, his prototype and plans, and perhaps kidnap Mr. Merchant himself and take him out of the country.

While preparing this briefing, I discover that there is now a second foreign power with several men in Missouri with the sole purpose of finding Mr. Merchant and evaluating his weapon. If they like it, they will attempt to buy it. If he won't sell, then they will simply steal it, probably kill Hirum Merchant, and return with the gun to their own nation. You must prevent this at all costs.

With the growing concern for finding new military weapons, our president feels that we must meet both of these threats by protecting Mr. Merchant.

You may requisition troops and weapons from any fort or army installation, including Fort Leavenworth just outside of Kansas City, Kansas. I have this day sent the fort commander a telegram authorizing such assistance from Fort Leavenworth.

Wire your receipt of these orders at once and wire me at any time you have need of assistance or direction and upon completion of the assignment.

There was the scrawled signature of General Warrenton at the bottom of the third sheet.

Canyon had sent a quick wire to Washington, put his magnificent palomino mount in a livery stable, and caught a night train to Kansas City. There was no way he could send his mount by train to Kansas City on such short notice. He bought a horse for the two-day ride to Short Creek, which had no stage service.

Now, laying in the brush up from the house, Canyon heard something. He looked back at the house. A figure ran silently toward the building, then went around it and soon found one of the Indian bodies. The warrior picked up the corpse, looked around, and then hurried into the darkness.

Canyon saw two other Osage retrieving their dead, then the stillness was complete again. He waited for a half-hour, and when the Indians didn't return, he closed his eyes and went to sleep. If anything moved within fifty feet of him, he would be awake instantly with his big army revolver in his fist.

Morning came suddenly on the plains with the sun bursting over the flatland horizon a hundred miles away, or so it seemed. Canyon was up and had slipped into his boots and gun belt, then shaved with cold water from his canteen. He sliced the whiskers off with a straight razor by feel. One of these days he was going to get a small metal mirror to carry with him.

He heard the house door open. Elizabeth came out, looked around, and went to the outhouse. She carried the revolver. He thought it was big enough to make a nasty hole. Canyon packed up his gear and tied it on his saddle, tightened up the cinch, and led the big bay mare down to the edge of the creek, where she drank her fill. He ground-tied her in some fresh grass and walked back to the house.

Elizabeth had just arrived at the door when he got there.

" 'Morning," he said.

She stared up at him and she looked as if she hadn't slept too well, "All right, all right, I've decided to lead you to where my pa is supposed to be. If all this is true you've been telling me, he might have left that spot as well, but we'll go and try to find him."

"Good, I was hoping you would say that."

"I've traveled before. I have a sack of food ready. Some bacon, eggs in a jar, two loaves of bread I baked yesterday, and some tins and dried goods. Couple of pots and a frying pan. You might find us a rabbit along the way. Breakfast first, flapjacks while we still have milk and syrup."

They left a half-hour later. She closed the door, locked it, and put the key on top the door frame. Then she turned and frowned at him, her pretty face tense. "Just so we get this straight. You are coming with me, not

18

the other way around. I know where we're going. I also have my thirty-two-caliber six-gun and I know how to use it. Right now I don't have any good reason to distrust you, and I hope it stays that way." She watched him a moment. "Any comments?"

"Only that you don't have to frown so much. It ruins your beautiful smile."

"Blarney will get you nowhere with me, Mr. O'Grady. Now let's ride."

They turned south and a little west. Canyon had admired the sleek way she fit into the ladies' riding trousers that she had on. They outlined her round little bottom delightfully. She wore a brown blouse and a light jacket and a straw hat with a wide brim with a tie under her chin.

She set a good pace down a country road, across a field, and toward the early-morning smokes of a village five miles away. They had just passed through a grove of trees when Canyon called sharply.

"Elizabeth, we've got company. Back to those trees, right now."

She saw the five men racing toward them across the field from the direction they had come. They were still three hundred yards away but coming at a gallop.

Canyon checked to see that the new Spencer carbine was still in his saddle boot, then kicked the bay in the flanks and surged into the brushline. He tied his mount, grabbed the Spencer, and ran to the edge of the brush.

Only two of them came straight on. The other three had circled around to the side.

"Damn," Canyon spat. Whoever it was planned on making a fight of it. So be it, Canyon growled to himself. He lifted the Spencer and sent a round over the heads of the two onrushing men, who were waving revolvers in the air. He'd find out quickly how serious they were about a fight.

2

Canyon fired the first rifle round over the pair of hard-riding men coming at the small patch of black willow, hickory, and hackberry woods. It was wasted. The two riders simply ducked lower and charged ahead.

Canyon's second shot brought down the lead horse with a round through the forehead, dumping the horse dead in a flying splash of dust and dirt. The rider rolled free and limped to a small hollow where he dropped out of sight.

Canyon was concentrating on the second horseman, who was closer now, and coming at them at a slight angle. Canyon fired once and missed. He figured that the round had gone high. The second time he aimed for the man's waist.

In the half-second it took the bullet to travel to the target the horse came forward and the round hit higher, jolting into the left chest of the rider, dumping him off the saddle to the ground, where he sprawled still and silent in death.

Canyon looked for the others. There were three more somewhere. He saw Elizabeth hunkered down behind a fallen tree near the horses. She had out her revolver. He motioned for her to stay there before he hurried past her at a crouch toward the other side of the small wood lot.

A horse blew noisily somewhere past the thick hackberry in front and to his left. Canyon froze behind a white ash and waited.

A footstep broke a branch to the right. He stared that way, saw some leaves move, and put a rifle shot into the still-fluttering leaves.

"Christ! Bastard winged me," a southern drawl bellowed into the woods.

Canyon watched the other way where the horse had talked. Nothing more. Then he heard saddle leather creak. The red-head sprang forward, running hard for the edge of the woods thirty yards ahead. He came out of the brush and saw two horses racing west no more than forty yards away.

He brought up the Spencer and tracked the best target, zeroed in on the man's back, led him a bit, and fired. He missed. Canyon levered in a new round and fired again. This time the man screamed, and surged forward, tangling with the reins and stirrup until he fell to the right side of his mount. His right foot had caught and twisted in the stirrup, and now his head bounced along on the ground as the frightened horse galloped with all his might away from the gunfire.

Canyon heard shooting on the other side of the woods: heavy rounds and a lighter sound that he figured was from Elizabeth's gun. He raced that way. There must have been one more rider he hadn't seen.

Canyon came toward the edge of the woods and found Elizabeth firing behind her log. Thirty feet away a rider had entered the woods and must have seen the horses. The rider fired again, and Elizabeth got off two shots. The man's horse screamed in pain and bolted for the open space.

The rider tried to control the horse but couldn't. Elizabeth's last shot sailed over his head, but the horse was in a panic then, racing out of the hackberry and sumac brush into the morning sunshine, away from what had caused him the pain and suffering.

It had been too brushy for Canyon to offer any help with his weapons. Now he rushed up to Elizabeth and grinned.

"That was some fine shooting."

"He came so close, and I know he saw the horses." She grinned. "Looks like the two of us did pretty good."

"We hurt them. The only reason they attacked must be that they know who you are. They wanted you to take them to your father."

"Probably." She winced.

"Are you all right?"

"Just dandy." She stood up and looked at him, then her face went white and she fainted, falling into the brush and wildflowers.

Canyon was beside her in one long stride. He lifted her head and straightened out one leg that was folded under her. That's when he saw the bloody stain. She had taken a round about midthigh.

"At least it's not fatal, lass," he said softly. He went to his horse and came back with a small packet of goods. In it was a slender bottle with a cork stopper, some tape, and some rolls of bandages.

He looked at her a moment, felt on the back of her thigh, and grunted when he touched the wetness of more blood. The round must have gone on through. Good.

Canyon reached for the belt around her riding pants, hesitated a minute, then shrugged. It had to be done. He undid the belt and the buttons down the front, then lifted her slender hips and pulled her pants down to her knees.

He noted the frilly white cotton drawers she wore, then saw the bullet hole in her left leg, higher than he thought. He looked at the back side. It was clear the slug had come out.

One thing Canyon knew was bullet wounds. He went to work quickly, washing off the wound with splashes from the bottle. It was a wash made of white vinegar, arrowroot, balm, and fuchsia. He'd used it for years.

Gently he cleaned both wounds and then put a square of cloth over them and taped them in place. Then he wrapped both bandages with strips of cloth from his kit until he was sure the cloth squares would stay in place. The white cloth went around her thigh and then was taped securely in place.

When he had the work done, he touched her face, then shook her shoulder gently.

"That hurts," Elizabeth said the second she woke up. She blinked, looked at him, then down at her bare thighs. Only then did she see the dressing. "Is it proper to be embarrassed while someone is bandaging up you leg?"

"If you need to be. I've seen a pretty woman's thighs before. No cause for alarm. The bullet went all the way through and out the other side. A little bit of Doc O'Grady's potion and you'll be good as new in two or three days."

"I didn't even know he hit me until it was all over. Is that strange?"

"Uncommon brave, I'd say. You can put your britches back on now, if you want to."

She gritted her teeth as she lifted her thighs and pulled up the pants. "I want to," she said. Elizabeth got her pants up and turned around as she buttoned them. When she tried to get to her feet, she fell against him.

"Sorry," she said as she steadied herself.

"I'm not complaining. You'll have to take it easy on that leg for a few days. Riding won't hurt it."

"That's good." She walked over to her roan, limping badly. At the saddlebag she took out a box of shells and reloaded her drained handgun with five fresh rounds. "I figured this would come in handy, but I never thought I'd shoot a horse. Poor creature. I guess if he ran off that fast, he must not be hurt too bad."

"Mostly scared. He'll be fine."

"How many were there?"

"Five of them. Two won't bother us anymore and we wounded one or two others. That will give them a thing or two to think about. They should know never to send a few boys to do a man's work.''

"You think they were the Americans? They looked like it.''

"Sounded that way from one of the men I wounded. Can't be sure. But they didn't look like they were trying to take any prisoners.''

"Did you . . .'' She looked away. "Did you kill any of them?''

"Yes.''

Elizabeth shuddered. She looked away and took several long, deep breaths.

"They were men trying to kill us.'' Canyon said. "Looks like the information about a threat to your father is correct.'' He let her get a tight grip on her emotions before he continued. "Maybe we should be on the road. The three attackers took off to the west. We're still aiming south, I'd guess.''

She nodded.

He went over and formed a step with his hand. She winced when she put her foot in it. Then quickly he swung her up and into the saddle. She rode a roan, a small animal, but sturdy and with a deep chest. It would keep up with his own bay in any kind of a run.

"You feeling all right? Well enough to ride?''

"Yes. It hurts, but you know that. Forget the leg. Let's go find Pa.''

"Good. You're a tough trooper.''

Elizabeth looked up at him quickly to see if he was teasing her. He wasn't. She nodded grimly.

"They found us here, they'll just come back and follow our tracks,'' Canyon said. "We'll have to do something to throw them off our scent.''

A mile on south they came to a six-inch-deep creek running the same direction they were going.

"We'll ride in the stream for a ways, a mile or two. That will give them fits.''

When they came out of the stream, they each left on

24

opposite sides, went a half-mile, and then back into the water for another mile.

"Now, we'll let these nags drink, then ride a couple of double circles that should really confuse them if they get this far. Never have seen a city boy who was a good tracker."

An hour later they made their circles and changed over and crossed back, and then headed for what seemed to be a well-traveled road. They rode onto it. By the signs of the traffic, in two or three hours there would be enough farm wagons over the ground to blot out their tracks for good.

"Down this road for about five miles and then we swing to the right over past El Dorado Springs," Elizabeth said.

"How much farther do we have to go?"

"We'll get there tomorrow. If nobody else shoots at us."

"How's the leg?"

"Still hurts. I guess you know that. You've been shot before. Is that right?"

"True, and you're correct, it hurts. But it's going to pain you less each day after today."

They rode ten more miles before she said they better find a place to camp.

"We can't go to an inn," he explained. "Somebody might see us and remember us for the next group looking for us. We'll keep out of sight as much as possible until we get there."

"Yes, I understand. But I would like to stop and rest. I haven't ridden a horse this far for a couple of years."

He found a wooded place near a stream and just off the well-traveled road. That day they had met farm wagons going to market with vegetables and one loaded with wheat. This was not stage-coach country. If you wanted to get somewhere in this part of eastern Missouri in 1860, you rode your own horse or walked.

The camp was on a little rise near a stream, and it gave them some protection and a good lookout position. Canyon figured one more smoke plume in this settled country wouldn't be noticed. He started a small cooking fire and ringed it with dry rocks. Early in his outdoors experience he had used wet rocks right out of the creek to form his fire ring. Later that night when he built up a bigger fire, one of the rocks had exploded.

He brought over the bag of food and the pots and pans from Elizabeth's horse. She sat down by the fire and winced. Then she sliced bacon and put it in the skillet. When she tried to get up on her knees to move the skillet, she dropped the skillet and the bacon into the fire. She grabbed her thigh and let out a screech of pain.

Canyon rescued the fry pan and Elizabeth sighed.

"Sorry. I'm usually not such a clumsy person," she said.

"You got shot. You're allowed one spilled pan of bacon a day for each shot."

She cut new bacon and this time got it fried. Quickly she made them thick sandwiches filled with two kinds of cheese half-melted by the hot bacon. There was coffee and, for dessert, half a can of sliced peaches.

"I was going to save the peaches, but today I need them," Elizabeth said. "Tomorrow we should find Pa and everything will be all right again."

"We hope."

She looked up quickly. "You don't think someone else has found Pa first, do you?"

"I hope not."

"Those men we fought with. Would they . . . would they shoot Pa?"

"No, I'm sure they wouldn't. They want him to finish the weapon so they can steal it."

"Oh, dear. He was just about done with it a month or so ago."

"Don't worry, Elizabeth. We'll get there first." He built up the fire a bit. "Bedtime. We'll be up at dawn and moving."

He got her blankets from her horse and she thanked him. She spread them out near the now brighter fire. He put his roll down across the fire from her.

She sat on her blankets, faced away from him, and pulled off her shirt. In the soft glow of the firelight he saw her breasts pushing against the chemise.

He stood and moved away a little as she slipped on a long nightshirt.

"I'm going to take a quick look around, a patrol of the area. Just to make sure we don't have any visitors."

She nodded. "Don't get lost," she said.

He made a quarter-mile circle around the camp, but neither saw nor heard anything that seemed to be out of place or dangerous.

When he came back, she was wrapped in her blankets, which she had moved over beside his.

When he sat down on his bed, she looked at him. "Canyon, I moved over here to be close to you. I'm . . . I guess that . . . Dammit, I'm scared! If you're close enough so I can reach out and touch you, I'll feel just ever so much better." She paused and then laughed. "I guess that means I'm more afraid of them out there than I am of you."

He couldn't see her face in the darkness but he wished that he could.

"There now, I've said it, but don't you get any ideas. I don't want to share your blankets. I just need to be nearby."

"I'd say that's my bad luck. If you really get frightened and need somebody to hold you, I'm right close."

'Don't worry, Mr. O'Grady. I've never been that scared in my life. Good night."

He listened to her breathing. She was sleeping within

27

a minute. He left his boots on, pulled off his gun belt, and kept the big Colt iron beside his right hand and the Spencer just beyond that. He was a light sleeper. Out in the open this way if an owl hooted within a quarter of a mile, he'd hear it and discount it as not dangerous before he woke up.

But if a moccasin hit the ground too hard, or a branch snapped back as someone passed within fifty feet, he'd be awake in a half a second with his six-gun in his steady right hand.

He woke once during the night, sat upright in bed, and the Colt came into his hand. Something to the left. He watched, but the faint odor of a white-tailed deer came first, then he saw them. A doe deer with twin fawns stepped daintily down a game trail he had seen on his scouting patrol. It was less than fifty feet to the side and led from the little rise down to the water.

One of the fawns wanted to root up a tender shoot, but the doe had caught the man scent and pushed the spotted little creature on down the trail. She turned and took one long look at Canyon where he sat in the darkness, then she continued along the path with a little twitch of her tail that showed she really wasn't afraid.

Morning came and a half-dozen songbirds greeted the dawn. In only two or three minutes he identified a bluebird, a cardinal, a bullfinch, and the imitative songs of the mockingbird.

He looked around before he moved. No one had a gun trained on him. There seemed to be no one in the area. He could sniff out no unusual odors. He could identify plainly the foreign scent of the face cream or rouge that Elizabeth wore.

An old trapper once told him that to be a good outdoorsman you had to have a nose as good as the animals you were trying to trap.

He raised up and checked farther, staring all the way around the small camp past the hazelnut and maple trees in this small grove. He found nothing dangerous.

Only then did he slide into his boots, strap on his gun belt and six-gun, and feel dressed. He figured they would have no fire this morning. A drink of cold water from the sparkling little creek, then some beef jerky and they would be on their way.

Elizabeth heard him by the time he had his bay packed up and ready to move. She scrambled upright, lifting the blanket to cover her chest. "We moving already?"

"About. You coming?"

"Yes, turn around while I get dressed."

He turned but caught a flash of her slipping the nightshirt off and reaching for her regular blouse.

He heard her stop rustling clothes.

"You want to . . . Do you need to look at my leg?"

"Always glad to look at a beautiful woman's bare thighs," he said with a small laugh.

"Don't get smart. One of the bandages slipped."

He moved over to her, knelt down, and saw that she had her riding pants down to her knees. The square of cloth holding over the entry wound on the top of her thigh had worked itself to the side, exposing some of the dark-blue hole where the slug entered her milk-white skin.

He unwrapped the long bandage, carefully pulled off the tape, and checked the entry wound. He could tell little yet. There had been no healing, but at least there was no sign of infection. He put some more of the vinegar wash on the wound, then put a fresh compress on it and bound both tightly with the strips of bandage.

"If that's too tight, let me know. Your foot will start to feel numb. We don't want that to happen. But it needs to be tight to keep it in place and keep you from bleeding to death."

She looked up sharply.

Canyon grinned. "Just fooling you, Elizabeth. No chance of that happening. I've never lost a patient yet."

"How many have you had?"

"Two, you and me."

A half-hour later they were riding again. There was pain on her face as they set off, then the motion and jolting of the animal's stride settled down and it seemed to keep the discomfort tolerable.

Determined to take her mind off her hurts, she looked over at the tall man with the red hair. "Canyon O'Grady, a most unlikely name. How did you get it, and why?"

"My mother gave me my name just as yours did for you."

"But Canyon is a rather strange first name."

"I was almost born in Ireland when my father ran into some trouble with the British constables. He was one of the ones who started the Young Ireland Movement and a fine friend of Finlan Lalor and Padraic Pearse. Having two friends like those put you on the British wanted-dead-or-alive posters.

"My mother knew they were coming to America, so she started reading books and looking at pictures of America. She decided Canyon should be my name since it symbolized for her the new, raw, wild land she was coming to. When I was baptized, the parish priest would not allow Canyon, so officially I'm Michael Patrick O'Grady. But my parents and my friends never called me anything but Canyon."

"And now you work for President Buchanan," she said. "That's quite a jump from immigrant to the White House."

"I just do odd jobs. I don't run the White House."

Elizabeth laughed. "I bet you could if they gave you the chance. You seem to do anything well that you take a try at. You must be an extremely expert special agent for the government to get this assignment."

"Haven't been fired yet."

"You're also stuck on yourself. No modesty at all."

"Modesty is a form of weakness. I try never to be

30

weak. Now, how much farther until we find your father?''

"This afternoon sometime. We're heading for a small settlement called Casper. It's on a river. More like a small stream. But it's there."

"I hope so. So far I can't see anyone following us. We might be lucky and have slipped away from your gun-toting admirers back there at the woods."

3

It was nearly three o'clock that afternoon before they came into the small settlement called Casper. A poorly painted sign on a crooked post at the outskirts of the place proudly proclaimed that Casper had a population of 347.

"This the place?" Canyon O'Grady asked the girl riding the roan beside him.

Elizabeth brushed back long blond hair and nodded. "Sure is. Pa and I been here two, three times before. He'd rent a house by the month down that way past the church."

"Can you find the place?"

"I can." She turned quizzical eyes upon him. "You want us to ride right up and say howdy?"

"Reckon that's the way polite people do things. Leastwise until we know we aren't welcome there."

She lifted her brows over pale-green eyes and shrugged. "Down this way a quarter-mile or so. Actually it's on the other side of town. Casper isn't all that big, as you can plainly see."

They rode past houses, down one street with more houses, bypassed the small business section, and came to a stop in front of a small house painted yellow. One struggling rose bush in the front yard had about given up the hope of getting any water. Its leaves were wilted. One bud had sagged on a limp stem.

"Right here," Elizabeth said, stepping down from her horse. They ground-tied the mounts, letting the reins hang to the thin Missouri soil, then both walked up to the front door. There was no porch. Hundreds of hands that had opened the door had left a two-foot-long dirty stain on the yellow paint.

Canyon knocked and waited. After a few moments he knocked again. Then he heard something inside. He nodded to the girl, who stood apart from him a little, giving him room to shoot if he had to.

The door opened slowly and a woman's face poked around the side and stared at them from brown eyes. She had brown hair and pink, full cheeks. She frowned slightly at them. "Do I know you?" she asked.

"I don't expect so, miss. My name is Canyon and this is Elizabeth. We're looking for a man named Hirum Merchant."

Her expression changed completely. "Land sakes, I've been looking all over creation for Miss Merchant here." The woman looked at Elizabeth. "Honey, your pa had to leave about two weeks ago. Said he wasn't getting his work done." She paused for a minute watching them, then she shrugged and came out from behind the door.

She was a hefty, plump woman. "Come in, come in. Your pa said if you showed up I was to be good to you." The woman was more than plump. Huge breasts nearly overflowed her blouse. Her arms were heavy as well, but her face, while full, was not disfigured with flesh. Canyon figured that ten years ago she had been a beauty. Her hair was cut short and must be naturally curly the way it sprang out in tight loops all over her head.

Elizabeth stared at the woman a moment. "We're in kind of a rush. You just tell me where Pa went and we'll push on without bothering you."

The woman shook her head. "Your pa would have my hide. Oh, land sakes, my name is Betty Jo." She caught Elizabeth's hand and urged her inside.

Elizabeth looked trapped but decided to be polite.

"Yes, Betty Jo, nice to meet you. This is my guide and friend, Canyon O'Grady."

Canyon nodded and touched the wide brim of his low-crowned, soft brown hat.

"Please to meet you, Miss Betty Jo," Canyon said. "But Elizabeth is right. We can't waste even an hour. We're late already, and it's gonna be old Ned to pay if we don't get to see her pa when we're supposed to."

"Business, business, business," Betty Jo said. "I know all about that, and there ain't a one of them businessmen who can't slow down a little or a meeting that can't be put off a day or two. You both just come in and rest a spell. I'll fix a good supper for you. Bet you've been eating around a smelly old campfire somewhere." Betty Jo looked at Elizabeth. "Bet you wouldn't mind having a good hot bath and washing that lovely blond hair, would you now, Elizabeth?"

"Well . . ." O'Grady began, then stopped.

"Maybe we can spare the time, Betty Jo. Just so we can get an early start. My pa did tell you where he was going from here, didn't he?"

"Of course. But I like to have company, so I'm gonna be selfish and not tell you until tomorrow. Bring in your bedroll and any kit you carry. We got beds aplenty in this place, and I'll fix you up with a fine supper." The woman laughed. "I'm a fine cook, as you can see. Guess I eat most of my work. But I haven't had company since you pa left. So, really, you'll be doing me a favor."

Elizabeth looked over at Canyon.

"I'd bet that Elizabeth would appreciate a good soft bed for a change, instead of that hard, cold ground. Wouldn't you now, Elizabeth?" Betty Jo prompted.

"Well, It would be nice, now that you mention it."

"Good, it's settled. Bring in your gear and I'll get the fire lit and some supper on the stove. I got me one of them kitchen ranges. The fancy kind with lids that come off on top and everything."

Canyon turned and headed for the horses. He took the reins, led them around to the back. He found a small shed, where he stabled them and took off their saddles. There was a small pile of hay to one side and he forked some over to the two horses, brushed them down a moment with a brush he found there, then picked up the blanket rolls and a small soft carpetbag Elizabeth had brought, and went inside.

As soon as he closed the kitchen door, Betty Jo handed him two buckets.

"Well's out there above the little barn a rod or so. Could you bring us some water? I think it's going to be for a bath."

"Mine?"

"Sure, Canyon, but you get seconds on the bathwater," Betty Jo said.

"I'll pass this time." He brought back the bathwater and poured it into a big copper boiler on the stove. Betty Jo worked in the small kitchen.

"How long has it been since Hirum left?" Canyon asked.

"Since he left? Oh, about a week or more now. He told me to stay here and he'd come back here when he's finished. He didn't say how long that would be."

"We really do need to find him. Did he leave a note or a letter for Elizabeth?"

"Afraid not. Hirum wasn't one to write notes much. But he sure did keep working. He was the workingest man I ever saw. He'd be in there all day and then again at nighttime. Some contraption thing he was tinkering with. Did tell me not to let anyone know about him, 'cepting, of course, if Elizabeth come around."

She rolled out a thin sheet of dough, then cut it into long strips for noodles. A minute later she dropped them into a pan of boiling water.

"Not hot enough yet. Liz might need some cold. Could I talk you into goin' down to the well for one more bucketful?"

He brought the water back and then knocked on a door where Betty Jo said Elizabeth was.

She called through the door. "Yes?"

"Need to talk."

"I'm not . . . not properly attired."

"Elizabeth, just open the door a crack so I don't have to shout."

She did, one pale-green eye staring at him.

"I get to bring in the bathwater," Canyon said with a leer.

"Stop it. What do you want to talk about?"

He lowered his voice to a whisper. "What about Betty Jo? Do you believe her?"

"Not for a minute," Elizabeth said, her voice also a whisper. "If Pa was to take a woman, she'd be like my mother, small and dainty, thin and about to blow away in a stiff wind. He never liked fat women."

"So?"

"So I'm going to have a bath. There's a lock on the door and a shutter inside on the window. I'll use them tonight. You keep your six-gun handy."

"I'll see what I can find out. You're sure this is the same house your pa used before?"

"I'm sure."

"Good. Enjoy your bath."

He went into the third bedroom, where Betty Jo had told him he could sleep. There was a bed and a workbench along one wall. He checked it and soon found metal shavings, where something had been filed down, and some scraps of canvas that had been neatly stitched with a double slot in it. He pushed his finger through the slots and wrinkled his brow.

Not exactly a cartridge belt, but something like it. He took a shell from the loop on his gun belt and pushed it into the slots. It fit snugly. He kept the scrap of canvas. Someone had done some calculations on a raw piece of lumber that lay on the workbench. There were two sets of figures with decimal points to four places. The numbers meant nothing to him.

"Water's ready," Betty Jo called from the kitchen.

Canyon went out and hefted the copper boiler with its wooden handles on both ends.

Betty Jo went to Elizabeth's door and knocked. "You decent? The water and the tub are here."

Elizabeth opened the door and stayed behind it as Canyon carried the boiler of water inside. Betty Jo put down a galvanized number-three washtub on the bare wood floor and Canyon slowly poured the hot water into the washtub.

By the time he had it poured in, Betty Jo was back with the bucket of cold water.

Elizabeth peeked from behind the door and Canyon saw part of the nightshirt he had spotted before.

"Come on, jump in," Canyon said with a grin.

"You get out!"

Canyon laughed and walked out of the room. He heard the bolt slide into place when the door closed.

Betty Jo watched Canyon a moment, then chuckled. "Yes, yes, a tough little lady. I'd wager you haven't had your way with that one yet, have you?"

Canyon simply raised his brows. "I wouldn't be much of a gentleman if I said either yes or no, now, would I?"

She shrugged. "Things ain't that complicated with me." Then, remembering the food on the stove, she lunged for the kitchen. "Don't you dare burn!"

An hour later, they sat down to the table and the dinner was delicious. Fried chicken, mashed potatoes, and chicken gravy with giblets, carrots and peas, and fresh-baked bread with wild-plum jam and buckets of coffee. For desert there was apple pie and fresh whipped cream.

Canyon pushed back from the table and groaned. "Haven't had a feast like that since I was in Chicago at a fancy restaurant. Something French."

"It was delicious, Betty Jo. You're right," Elizabeth said. "It's a lot better this way than squatting around a campfire picking meat off the bones of a rabbit." She smiled at the larger woman. "Betty Jo, how long has it been since Pa left here?"

"Like I told Canyon, little more than a week he's been gone. Figure he'll be back in a couple more days."

Elizabeth helped do the dishes, then announced she was tired. "Been a long day for me," she said. Canyon had a chance to whisper to her about her leg. She said she had bandaged it again after the bath. The wounds looked about the same, at least no angry red places.

Betty Jo and Canyon played two draws of dominoes, then went to bed themselves. There was no bolt on the inside of Canyon's door. He didn't mind. He placed the room's one straight-back chair an inch from the door, slid out of his boots, pants, and shirt, and crawled into the bed in his summer underwear.

Canyon figured it would take an hour. He missed it by half an hour. The door to his room opened slowly half an inch, then pushed in sharply, scraping the chair along the wooden floor.

"Damn!" Betty Jo said as she slipped past the chair and closed the door. She turned up the wick on a lamp she carried and frowned at Canyon. "You were expecting Indians to scalp you?"

"Expecting you," he said.

"Well, good. Best news I've had all day." She put the lamp down on the bench and sat down on the bed. She wore a light cotton nightgown.

Canyon lay where he had been, his hands behind his head. "I'm feeling a bit sleepy," he said.

Betty Jo bent down and kissed his lips. Her big breasts pushed against his chest. "You're not surprised I'm here?"

"Just that you came so early."

"Makes a longer night of it that way." She crossed

her arms and pulled the nightgown up and over her head, throwing it across the room at the door.

There was a lot of Betty Jo. Watermelon-sized breasts surged out, sagging from their own bulk. Her pink nipples were as big as his thumb, already swollen and throbbing. Large areolae glowed pink around the sentinels. He had been wrong about her body: it was not so much fat as thick and solid flesh.

"You like what you see, grab a mouthful," Betty Jo said with a slight drawl.

"You're the direct type, I'd say."

"Direct enough." She bent and kissed him again, then lifted and let one breast dip to his mouth. He nibbled at the nipple, then caught a larger mouthful and chewed tenderly.

"Oh, damn, you know how to please a lady." She pushed the blanket off him and pulled at his drawers. A moment later she snaked them off his feet.

"Oh, yes, the good part of a man. Hey, not even a little excited yet?"

"I been down the road before, woman. I'm not fourteen."

She giggled, then a belly laugh escaped. "I can tell you don't get worked up easy. Now that's my job. Hell, I been wet down below since I first opened the damn door this afternoon and saw you. Them slender hips and that bulge at your crotch. Makes me get all goosebumpy and my little slot just twitching and hopping. By now I'm hot as a two-dollar pistol just waiting to go off."

Her hand found his crotch and she worked on him, teasing, pulling, massaging, and then she grinned.

"See, see! Billy Jo ain't lost her touch. Always could get the cold ones warmed up good and proper. You want the first time real fast, and then we can figure out some new moves for the second and third and fourth and fifth. I got to have me at least five times tonight or I might die."

Canyon caught both her breasts and rubbed them. He had never seen larger ones in his life.

"Five sounds about right, if you can last. Thought you said you were sleepy?"

"That was sleepy as in wanta-be-fucked-sleepy."

She went to her knees beside his crotch and bent and kissed his erection. "Oh, yes!" Betty Jo moaned. "I still get a boot out of a little mouth-organ music. First time I ever did it I was fourteen and I kept climaxing for fifteen minutes. The poor boy I was with got scared thinking I was dying. It was his first time with a girl and he pulled on his pants and ran through the field all the way home. I nearly did die, laughing."

She didn't talk then for a few minutes, taking him deep and full in her talented mouth, touching some nerves he hadn't felt for a long time. He reached down and pulled her away.

He pushed her on her back and she grinned. "Anytime you're ready, cowboy. I'll give you a ride you won't forget, guaranteed."

Canyon dropped between her raised knees and thrust into Betty Jo in one clean stroke, bringing a yelp of surprise and pleasure from the woman. Then it was a battle, a fight between two evenly matched opponents, each determined to outgun the other. A clashing, thrashing, pumping contest that ended only when both of them brayed in release and then fell on the bed exhausted.

Vaguely he realized something was wrong. It wasn't the way it should be. Even in his climax he was on the defensive, counting on survival instincts. He watched her as she moved. Her hand fumbled under the mattress for a moment, then came up. He sensed more than saw that she had something in her hand. Then it came into the light of the kerosene lamp.

Before he could call out, the butcher knife she held slanted down toward his back where he still lay on top of her. His right arm flailed upward to deflect the blow.

At the same time a gun roared in the closed room and it sounded like an army artillery piece going off right next to him. Blood splattered on him, warm and wet.

Betty Jo bellowed in pain.

The knife clattered to the wooden floor.

Canyon surged away from the woman, pushing to his feet and standing beside the bed, naked. Elizabeth stood two steps into the room in her white nightgown, which tried to hide her womanly curves but didn't have a chance of doing so. Her breasts pushed out the top delightfully.

Betty Jo sat up on the bed, holding her left forearm with her right hand. Blood seeped out from between her fingers.

"Bitch! You shot me," Betty Jo roared.

"Exactly, and the next one goes in your heart if you move again," Elizabeth said evenly. She held the little six-gun in both hands, arms extended, feet spread. Someone had taught this girl how to shoot.

Canyon stood there watching the naked woman. "I think it's about time you start telling us the truth, Betty Jo. You weren't here with Hirum. He likes thin, small women. You were here waiting for us. Who are you working with, the five-man gang we shot up yesterday?"

"Oh, God, it hurts! Stop the bleeding. Stop the damn bleeding. Stop the damn bleeding, then I'll tell you everything I know."

"No," Elizabeth said. "You talk right now or I'll shoot you again. Did you kill my father?"

'No, God, no! I never even saw him. They told me your name, told me to wait here for you. Then I was to . . . to incapacitate whoever came with you, and they'd come by and find out from you where your dad was. That's it.''

"You're working with somebody. Who is it that set you up here to wait for us?"

"I'm not sure. Some smooth-talking guy met me in the saloon and said I could earn a hundred. Now stop the bleeding."

Canyon grunted and Elizabeth swung down the revolver. He ripped up a sheet on the bed and wrapped it ten times around her arm where the bullet had gone through the fleshy part, missing the bone.

"Have a doctor treat that tomorrow," Canyon said. He looked at Elizabeth. "How did you know she had a knife?"

"I saw her looking at you during dinner like she wanted to eat you up. It wasn't hard. I saw her go to your room. Then I just listened. I slid the door open when the wild sounds stopped. I got here just in time." Elizabeth waved one hand at him. "Now, would you mind putting on your pants."

They let Betty Jo dress as well, then tied her to a chair for the rest of the night.

"What now?" Elizabeth asked.

"We try to find out where your father went from here. This was his workroom. I found some metal and shavings and some canvas. Also some figuring on a board."

They looked around the room a little.

"He might have left something here to tell you where he went next."

"We used to have a kind of code we used," Elizabeth said. "Jumbled words that wouldn't make any sense to anyone else."

Canyon looked up quickly. "Like these over here?" He took her to the far end of the workbench, where some cardboard had been tacked to the wood. It held half a dozen words that were garbled and misspelled.

Elizabeth laughed softly. "Oh, yes, that's just what I mean. Exactly like that." She looked at the strange words and then glanced up and ginned. "Good. Now I know exactly where Pa is headed and which way he'll go. We can start after him first thing in the morning."

4

Elizabeth and Canyon had left Betty Jo tied to a heavy chair in her bedroom. There was no chance she could get away before morning. Elizabeth was still in her cotton nightgown and not at all embarrassed by it. She stood with her head high, her eyes bright from the excitement. Now they were in the small living room and she looked at Canyon.

"I'm sorry about bursting into your bedroom that way. I had no right to do that, since I strongly suspected that you were . . . let's say 'occupied' with that woman. Betty Joe is certainly a direct person, isn't she?"

"Yes, direct. She was looking for the best way to kill me. Figured she had it worked out. Until you shot her."

"I should have let you handle it. But when she slipped into your room I wasn't sure if you were awake. Then I heard some talk and then it got all quiet. When I peeked in, I saw her get that knife out from under the mattress."

"Sure you weren't looking at what was happening on top of the mattress?"

"Mr. O'Grady! What you do with . . . with common women you associate with is certainly not my affair. I can assure you that I'm not a curious young girl about that sort of behavior."

"Good. I'm glad to know at least a little personal information about you. Thanks. And thanks for using that six-gun of yours. Somebody taught you how to shoot. Even though I swung at her, she might just have got lucky and put that big knife into my back."

"She didn't. So forget it. We better get some sleep. Leave at dawn?"

"I'll try to be ready," Canyon said with a grin. He stared at her again. "I really like that nightgown. It's my favorite of the things I've seen you wear."

She frowned. "Forget it, Canyon. This was strictly an emergency. I didn't have time to dress properly. Don't get your hopes up, because I'm not another Betty Jo. Besides, I still have my little persuader here." She waved the revolver, then turned and walked quickly into her room, closed the door, and threw the bolt hard so he could hear it.

Canyon chuckled and went back to his own bed.

They left a half-hour after dawn. Canyon untied half of the strips of cloth that bound Betty Jo to the chair.

"You can get the rest undone before noon and go see the local sawbones," Canyon told her. "You're damn lucky you aren't dead. If that had been me at the door instead of Elizabeth, you'd have a new and bloody opening in the side of your head."

Betty Jo wailed at him. "You can't leave me here like this. I might bleed to death."

"Your friends should be along directly, " Canyon said. "They'll be glad to help you loose if you can't do it yourself."

Canyon and Elizabeth sat on their horses outside the house, and Elizabeth pointed south. "Pa said he was heading for Nevada, the town here in Missouri. He said the place has a good gunsmith he knows and he needs to use some of the man's equipment."

"He say anything else in your coded message?"

"Only that if I came this way, he would see me in Nevada. The little town is over near the western border of the state and maybe fifteen miles on south of here."

They rode for a moment before Canyon turned toward the town. "I need something before we head out," he said.

"What do we need?"

"A stage ticket for you back to Short Creek. It's getting too dangerous down here for you. I want you safe back home. I know, I said you could come along, but that was before people started getting killed. Now you're heading home."

"You forget there aren't any stages through here. None at all. You really want me riding alone all the way back to Short Creek?"

"With that gun, you won't have any trouble. I'm not taking you with me any farther. You've been helpful, I admit. But comes a time when I go on alone. That time is now. You turn around and head out of town to the north. I'll be watching you until you're out of sight. Soon as I get this straightened out, I'll stop by with your pa at your place in Short Creek."

"No, I—"

He held up his hand, stopping her words. "Hey, pretty lady. I've never been real good about holding my temper. I'd rather not demonstrate my failing. You get that perky little bottom of yours up the road before I have to spank you. I don't use words lightly, lass. Off you go!"

She watched him a minute. "I've got all the food."

"I won't starve. I've lived off the land before."

"Dammit, Canyon . . ."

He shook his head. "No. Forget it. I don't want to see you again until this is over. That way there's no chance of you getting hurt. Now get out of here, Merchant, before I get angry with you."

"Not even a kiss good-bye on the cheek," she said, smiling now.

"Not even. Get out of here!"

She turned her horse's head then and cantered away from him, heading north. He sat there for a while and watched her. Twice she turned and looked back at him.

When he couldn't make out her slim form sitting the horse, he turned and galloped for a quarter of a mile south. He eased up and found a sign that pointed to the west with the crudely scrawled word: NEVADA. He was on the right track.

Twice that morning he asked how to get to Nevada and was told he was on the right road. Three times he had stopped and watched his back trail from cover—the last time from a patch of flowering dogwood. He waited fifteen minutes and found no sign that the girl was following him. He didn't quite trust her, but by the end of the morning he decided she had agreed with his reasoning and was on her way home.

He crossed two small streams and rode faster. One man said Nevada was less than ten miles ahead then. He ate up the miles, stopped at the next creek, and let his big bay drink and munch on some grass. He took out a sack of beef jerky from his saddlebag and chewed on a piece half an inch wide and eight inches long. He had put the jerky in his saddlebags when he left Kansas City.

An hour later he rode into Nevada. It had more than a thousand people, a sign said, and it sported a fairly respectable business district. He had to ask only one man wearing a gun to learn where the gunsmith in town was.

"That'd be Merce Green, over at Green's Hardware," the man said. "Best damn gunman in the state, I say."

Canyon walked across the street, went in the front door of the hardware store and let the screen door slam. Nobody seemed to be inside. No customers, no clerks. He went to the back by the kegs of nails and looked around.

It was a fine hardware store, stocked with the goods that farmers and ranchers in this area needed. A blanket covered a door into the back.

"Anybody here?" Canyon called loudly.

There was no answer. He pushed the curtain aside and went through with his six-gun in hand. To the left against the far wall he saw a board that held a dozen different guns hanging on nails, each with a white tag.

The gunsmith's workbench. He went in that direction and stopped suddenly. A body lay just below the bench. It had a neat round hole in the forehead and an ugly black circle around it from powder burns.

Someone had executed the gunsmith. Why?

Canyon heard someone come in the front of the store. Canyon headed for the back door that opened outside.

A voice called from the front. "Hey, Merce, you tinkering with them guns again? Sheriff Warnick here. You back there, Merce?"

Canyon stepped out the back door and closed it without a sound. At once he saw what he was hunting. In the soft dust of the alley behind the hardware-store door were fresh horse prints. At least three sets. The animals had come up the alley, been tied to one side, and now boot prints showed where the riders had got off and back on. Then the three sets of hoof prints headed out of the alley at a much faster rate.

Canyon ran down the alley. He got to the end before anyone called to him. Quickly he went around the block to where he had tied up his horse. He mounted and rode back to the alley mouth and checked for the three sets of fresh horseshoe prints. He found them. There wasn't much traffic along here. The tracks headed to the east.

They went across the street and into the next ally. When he looked up, he saw a lone horseman coming toward him from the other end of the alley. The sun glinted off his chest and Canyon figured it had to be the sheriff or a deputy.

Canyon pulled up and waited for the lawman.

"Going somewhere?" the man asked Canyon.

"Reckon I'm heading out of town, Sheriff."

The man nodded, pushed up his hat, and frowned.

"Seems like you got to be the stranger Josh said he directed into the hardware store."

"That's right. Went in to see Merce Green, but three men beat me to him. Those are their tracks you're riding over right now."

The lawman moved his mount to the side of the alley. He was about fifty, had probably done his share of gunfighting. Now he had found a spot to slow down and ease up a little.

"Suppose you can prove you didn't shoot Merce."

"Not rightly, Sheriff. Except I'm not riding three horses and my six-gun hasn't been fired recently. Welcome to check on it."

The sheriff walked his horse closer, stared at Canyon a minute, then shook his head. "Nope, don't figure I need to do that. Would appreciate your letting me know what you find. Nevada ain't very good about sending out posses."

"One way or another, I'll get word back to you."

"Be obliged. You have a name? Mine is Jonathan Warnick."

"Canyon O'Grady. I'll be in touch."

Canyon rode on down the alley, checking the prints. The horses were moving faster now. Did the three killers get out of the old gunsmith where Hirum had gone? Probably, or they wouldn't have killed the man.

The plain trail continued out of town, then swung to the west again. Maybe they were heading into the Kansas Territory. Folks there hoped to be admitted to the union in 1861, but that was no sure thing with the slavery issue such a big fight right then in Congress.

Canyon rode another three miles. The tracks kept to the road for a while, then angled across some open prairie land as if the riders were taking a shortcut to another road or another town. Settlements in that western section of Missouri were few and scattered.

The tracks led into a small section of walnut and maple trees surrounded by hackberry. He sat and looked at it for a while. It could be a trap. He spurred his big bay around the edge of the copse to the far side and slowed and watched the virgin ground cover carefully.

Soon he picked up the three sets of prints heading farther west. No trap. On a whim he rode back into the woods to see if the trio had paused there long enough to camp or set a fire. He found nothing and was almost at the far side of the woods when he saw a rider following his own trail. The rider dropped into a swale and went out of sight.

Curious, Canyon moved back into the hackberry until he couldn't be seen from the outside; he carved a small viewing port of his own and waited.

A few minutes later the rider came out of the swale and rode hard for the woods. Canyon faded back father to get a few more substantial walnut trees between him and the rider and waited.

Soon the rider charged into the brush, then stopped. The rider was small, then O'Grady took a second look and swore softly.

Canyon charged toward the person on the horse, who fumbled for a weapon. "Steady," he shouted. "Don't draw that iron!"

The rider looked up and he saw the pale-green eyes and the grin of Elizabeth Merchant.

Canyon pulled to a stop beside her with his leg touching hers. "What in hell are you doing following me? Don't you know that's a damn good way to get yourself killed?"

"I wanted to come with you," she said, her chin held stiff and proud. "He's my pa who is in danger, and I have the right to help find and protect him."

"Oh, glory and three Irish saints! Are you tired of living? Didn't you see the gunsmith back in town?"

"No, but I heard what happened. There were men running all over the place. I'm sorry for Mr. Green."

"Just the way I'll be sorry for you when you're laid out in a pine box and in a three-foot grave. Damned sorry, but that won't bring the sparkle back to those bewitching eyes, or the bloom to your pink cheeks, now, will it?''

"No. But still I'm coming. You can't stop me. He's my father, not yours."

Canyon glared at her for a moment. "You're not going to be sensible about this, are you?"

She grinned. "No, Canyon, I'm not. I'm going to be emotional and cry all over you if you even think about sending me home again. I cry real good."

Canyon reached out and touched her shoulder. "You've been shot once, isn't that enough?"

"No, not until my pa is warned and safe."

He shrugged. "All right, but you'll be following my orders. Agreed?"

"Yes, sir," she said, offering him a salute.

"Let's get moving. We have a trio of killers to catch. They shot Mr. Green, I'm sure, right after he told them where you pa is headed next. We follow them and then we find your pa. It's the only trail we have left."

They rode. He set a blistering pace, but Elizabeth tightened her pretty mouth and kept up with him on the sturdy little roan.

All afternoon the trail wound to the northwest. Once the trio had stopped, made a fire and boiled coffee, and had hot beans and hard crackers to eat.

He found the cans of the beans and an empty cracker package.

"Stayed here maybe an hour, then moved on. They're not real outdoorsmen. Notice that they didn't even bother to put out their campfire, just let it burn down and go out. We could have had a range fire out here that way."

As they rode, Elizabeth came up so their legs nearly touched. "O'Grady, tell me about yourself. You came here with your father at a tender young age. What did your father do?"

"He went with the Irish work gangs that helped build

the railroads in the East. But as I grew up, I knew for certain that I didn't want to be another Irish construction man. I needed something with more adventure in it. So, when I was old enough, I came West, into the new frontier.''

"You never went back to Ireland?''

"Twice, as a matter of fact. Went with father both times, partly to disguise his real intentions. We stayed for two years on each trip.''

"That was so your father could get back into the Irish revolution, wasn't it?'' Elizabeth asked.

"He never told me for sure, but I suspect you're right. He bundled me off to a monastery with a group of priests known for their wisdom and learning. They struggled to pound some learning into my thick Irish head.

"Anything that penetrated is their fault, not a bit of my own doing. But I'm glad for all the toil and sweat they made me do over the poets and writers and historians and adventurers of long years ago.''

A half-mile ahead the trail faded to nothing. It simply vanished on hard rock. They circled and found it beyond the outcropping of hard flat rock.

"At least they don't think they're being followed. That would have been an ideal place to confuse their trail. They simply rode straight across the hard spot in the same direction. They can't be more than about four hours ahead of us.''

"How can you tell?'' Elizabeth asked.

"You really want to know?''

"Yes, of course.''

"By the heat of the horse droppings we've been finding. I can tell by the appearance as well. See, I didn't think you would be that excited about it.''

"If it helps us capture the men, or stop them from harming my pa, I'm all for it.''

He talked her into telling about her youth as they rode. The day was sunny but fading as she talked.

"I don't remember much of my mother. I've seen tintype pictures of her. She was shorter than I am, but about the same coloring, Pa says. She died of the pox when I was five. She was the only one in town to get sick, and nobody could figure how. She hadn't been on a trip or talking with strangers. We know you get the smallpox from other people.

"Anyway, Pa and I were alone, so we had to make do. His sister came and stayed with us for a while, but then she got married and left. Pa raised me. We're the only family we have left, just him and me and his sister in Chicago.

"He ran a little gunsmithing business in the edge of Kansas City, Missouri, for a lot of years. Then, when I was seventeen, he got this idea about his fast gun, and he spent so much time on it his customers went to other gunsmiths.

"That was when we moved to a little town where he was the only gunsmith. Then we got by. Two years ago he quit fixing other people's guns and worked all the time on his 'invention,' as he called it. He showed me a little about it, but I don't hardly know one part of a gun from another. So I can't really help you with what Pa is making.

"Last year he took gunsmithing jobs twice so we could pay our bills and get enough to eat. He's determined to finish his project and says that then we won't have to worry about money anymore. We can move to a big city and I can go to a school or take piano lessons or dancing lessons, or study painting, or just do anything I want."

"What do you want to do, Elizabeth? If you could do anything you wanted to do."

"I don't know. First we have to find Pa, don't we?"

The big red ball of fire rimmed the horizon, and he turned into a small grove of trees that had a lot of wild-cherry trees and some persimmon and hickory. The brushy part would hide them for the night. They weren't

53

near any roads and Canyon wondered if they were over the line into Kansas Territory yet. Close.

He left the horses with their saddles on in case they had to leave in a rush. He loosened the cinches on both, let them drink their fill at a small stream, and then picketed them where there was some spring grass.

"Fire?" Elizabeth asked.

Canyon had seen no pursuit all day. He didn't even know if anyone was following or hunting them now. He shrugged. "Why not? If they are out there, they'll probably find us either way. At least we can have some better food this way. What are we having for supper?"

She looked up with a frown. "Canyon, you sent me home with all the food, remember. I thought you were eating off the land." She laughed softly, watching him.

"Woman, I just might tie you to a tree all night."

"I repent and will fix you some supper. Bacon is gone and so are the potatoes. I can heat up a can of beans and cut the last of that loaf of bread. If you find any little blue spots on it, just cut them out. Oh, and coffee. Can you find a nice flat rock I can set the pot on?"

"Sounds like a feast. I'll take a look around."

A shot slammed through the dusk as three men stepped out of the brush, all carrying rifles.

"You vill not take the step anywhere," the biggest of the three shouted in a heavy German accent. The rifles were aimed directly at Elizabeth and Canyon.

5

The big man scowled at them, his rifle holding steady. "Ve have no vish to harm you, kind people. In the vilderness we just protect ourselves, no?"

He came closer and lowered the rifle, but the other two men who had not spoken kept their weapons trained on Canyon. "My name is Hans and I am looking for a young lady. She is blond, yes, such as your goodself, missy."

"Afraid you have the wrong end of the stick, friend," Canyon said pleasantly. "We ain't got nothing worth stealing, and we're on our way into town. Just me and my wife here. I'm Jimmy Johnson and this is my good wife, Geraldine."

Elizabeth looked at him sharply. He put his arm around her and pulled her up and kissed her firmly on the lips, then let her down. Canyon laughed. "See, we ain't been married but two weeks, and Geraldine here ain't quite used to me yet."

"No, no, no. You be Elizabeth Merchant, missy. You have the letter ve need. Ve look through the goods unless you give us letter."

"Like I said, friend, you've got the wrong people." Canyon moved a step toward the big German when a rifle shot jolted through camp and tore into the ground a foot in front of Canyon's foot.

"You vill stay still or get shot, makes no difference me." He walked to their bedrolls and the sack of possibles and food and shook out everything. He did not find what he was searching for.

When he was sure, he came back and reached toward Elizabeth but she pulled back.

"Must search you, missy."

"No!" She swung her hand to slap him, but the big German caught her wrist easily, twisted her arm behind her back, and with his other hand felt her body around her waist, then up and over each breast and between them.

Hans shook his head and pushed her away. He looked at Canyon. "Open out pockets," he said.

"Look, crazy German. I told you we don't have any letter. Now just get—"

The German pulled a six-gun and cocked it in one sure motion and the deadly black hole of the muzzle pressed against Canyon's chest.

"Open out pockets," Hans said again.

Canyon moved his hands slowly to his pockets, grabbed the inside of each, and pulled them outward. Everything inside fell out, a two-dollar gold piece, a small folding penknife, a quarter, and a packet of matches. He had no back pocket.

The German motioned for Canyon to pick up the things. He backed off a dozen feet. "Vell, maybe the mistake. Girl looks like one we hunt. Same hair. Age right."

Elizabeth laughed. "That's crazy. There are fifty girls in this area about my age with blond hair. A lot of Germans and Swedes around here."

"You just come from town Nevada?"

"Sure, to get where we're going you have to pass through there," Canyon said. "Now, if you don't mind, we were trying to set up our camp for the night."

"Yes, sorry. Wrong missy. Much sorry." Hans turned and started to leave. "How you say, no feelings hard?"

"Yeah, yeah, forget it." Canyon saw the rifles had

56

been put away, but the speaker still held his six-gun in hand. The three men backed away from the small cleared place and then vanished into the brush.

Canyon held up his hand to quiet Elizabeth before she said anything. He pointed at her to get her six-gun and stay there. He drew his revolver and ran to the nearest tree in the direction the Germans took. A few seconds later he faded into the brush.

Five minutes later he was back.

"They had left horses at the edge of the brush. Evidently they had followed us a ways, but not all the way from Nevada. Did you see them in town when you were there?"

"No." She held up her finger and wagged it at him as if chastising a child. "That was a sneaky way to kiss me."

"Sure it was. But didn't you like it? I didn't hear any screaming and you didn't do a whole lot of struggling to get away."

"Of course not. I was only going along with the act to make them think we were married."

"Must have worked."

"Be serious. Could they be the three men who killed that gunsmith, the one we're following? Maybe they just doubled back."

"Not a chance. The ones we're tracking got what they wanted from that gunsmith, that's why they could kill him. They know where they're going."

"Maybe so . . ." She scrunched her face into a frown. "But I still think it was a sneaky trick to kiss me that way. Why don't you admit that you enjoyed it?"

"Enjoyed it? Of course I enjoyed it. Every time I get to kiss a pretty woman, I take the pleasure. I also liked the idea that we were fooling them. This invention of your father's could be tremendously important to the United States military. It looks like our reports that the Germans were highly interested in it are true. They rode back toward Nevada. Let's hope they keep going that direction.''

"What should we do now, stay here or move on?''

"They might be watching. Let's cook ourselves some supper on a fire, then I'll have an idea. It should be dark by then and they won't know if we're still here or not. I think we convinced them, but the German mind is hard to figure.''

They had supper, then cleaned up the dishes in the nearby stream.

Elizabeth looked at Canyon. "Now?''

"Now we fill up bedrolls and make it look like we're still here. Then we take one blanket each and slip off in the dark and wait and see what happens. My guess is that we'll have some company before long.''

The dummies evidently sleeping by a small fire looked realistic enough from the edge of the brush. Canyon and the girl went off fifty feet so they could still see the campsite, and sat down and pulled the blankets around them.

"You sure this is a good idea?'' Elizabeth asked.

"Better than getting shot to death around the fire.''

"Warmer down there.''

"I'm willing to share my blanket with you, pretty lady.''

"You also steal kisses. How can I trust you?''

"You can't. That's what makes it even more exciting.''

"I'll just be chilly for a while, thank you all the same,'' Elizabeth said. She leaned against an oak tree and closed her eyes.

He heard her shifting positions for a few minutes, then her breathing evened out and became deep and regular. She was asleep.

Canyon yawned but looked down through the trees and brush at their campfire. It blazed up for moment as one of the new sticks caught fire. He could spot the two blanket rolls.

Before they had come here to wait out any prowlers, he had moved the horses. He put one on each side of the little camp about twenty yards inside the brush from the open country. He was hoping the horses would act as watchdogs for him.

After what he figured was two hours, he came fully awake from his half-sleep. One of the horses had nickered and was answered by another mount somewhere to the left.

Horse talk! Yes, someone was coming from the left. Canyon grabbed his Spencer and moved quietly down the slope twenty feet to where he had a good open field of fire on the camp. Then he waited.

It was another ten minutes before he heard them coming through the brush. They were not as careful, since they must have figured their victims would be asleep by now.

He saw a shadow develop at the edge of the clearing where there hadn't been one before. The shadow grew into a man and he stood and walked silently to the small blanket roll that should be Elizabeth.

Another shadow came and stood over the larger blanket roll. The man at the larger body form held a sixgun and now he fired four times into the blanket as the other man waited for reaction from the second blanket.

No reaction came. A third man ran into the camp and they shouted at one another in German. One tore apart the blanket rolls and found only brush under the blankets.

Before they could run, Canyon sighted in on one man and fired, whipped the trigger guard on the Spencer down, levering out the spent round and chambering in a new live cartridge.

He fired four times as fast as he could. One man went down, another screamed in pain, and then the forms darted into the brush before he could fire again. He sent four more rounds into the thin growth where they had vanished, then drew his six-gun and ran as silently as he could through the brush following the bushwackers.

When he got to the edge of the brush, he saw two horses galloping to the east and away from the patch of woods there on the western Missouri flatlands.

By the time Canyon got back to the campsite, Elizabeth was already there.

"They tried to kill you in your sleep, without a word of warning," she blurted. "How could they do that?"

"They must be working on orders. They kill on demand, for money."

Canyon squatted near the body of the German. He hadn't moved. Canyon touched his neck. There was no pulse. Already the body was starting to cool. He went through the man's pockets, found ten dollars in gold, but no letters, no cards or wallet or anything to identify him.

"They were screaming at one another in German, so it's a good guess they were the trio we met before, earlier tonight."

"But they were so polite, almost nice then." Elizabeth shook her head in the dim firelight. "I just don't understand." She shivered. "Now another man is dead. I'm . . . I'm not used to this killing. Before I met you, I'd never seen a dead body besides my mother. Is this all necessary?"

"It is if we want to stay alive, and if we want to help your pa. I know you do. This gun of your father's is of great importance, both here in this country and in Europe. It must work, and it must fire so fast that everyone is excited about it. We wish he would have come to us early so we could have protected him."

"Pa said he wasn't going to beg. Evidently he had written a letter to the army last year and never heard anything back from them."

"Yes, that sounds like the army. Well, pack up, it's time for us to be moving on. As long as we're riding, nobody can kill us in our sleep."

"How do we know which way to go?"

"We'll head the same general direction the tracks were taking. There must be a small town ahead. Maybe your father is looking for a gunsmith with a machine or some tools that the one back there didn't have. If we lose the tracks tonight, we'll circle tomorrow until we find them."

They rode. He took his bearings from the stars and kept on the general course they had been on during daylight. After an hour they stopped to water the horses and he showed her how to tell time by the Big Dipper and the North Star. He had to stand next to her and point, and she looked up his arm and her face came close to his. It was just after ten P.M.

She found the star and understood but didn't move away at once. "No more stealing kisses," she said softly.

"How about a gift of one?" Canyon asked.

"That's entirely different," Elizabeth said, turning more toward him.

He kissed her lips softly, then eased away. Her hand went around his neck and pulled him back to her and she kissed him again, warmly, letting it linger.

When she backed away from him in the moonlight, she was smiling. "Now, Mr. O'Grady, isn't that just ever so much better than being a kiss thief?"

"Ever so much better, aye, it is that, lass. But right now we best get back in the saddle if we want to make any distance tonight."

An hour later he touched her shoulder and they stopped.

"Smell anything?" he asked.

She frowned, sniffed. "Yes, wood smoke. But I might not have noticed it. Where from?"

"Upwind," he said. "If it's downwind of you, you can't smell it. Let's go take a look."

They rode slowly now, and he tied neckerchiefs around the muzzles of their horses so they wouldn't do any horse talking with any mounts that might be in the woods just ahead.

He left her at the edge of the brush with the horses and worked his way silently forward.

It took him a half-hour to get to the fire. It was burning brightly and two men sat near it, talking. He couldn't make out what they were saying. They were speaking in English. He worked closer.

"Damn, we have to find this guy," the larger of the two men sitting near a bright fire said. "You realize the kind of profits we could make? So we have to hire some gunmen. Who cares? You and I could come out of this with an invention worth ten or twelve million dollars. We would never have to work again. We could leave millions to our children. We could establish a dynasty of wealth and power."

The smaller man on the other side of the fire frowned. He had a thin face and what looked to be a full beard. "Then we won't just be partners with this guy?" the smaller man asked.

"Hell, no. We grab it, and when we're sure we know all about it, we dispose of this Merchant guy and take his gun as our own. We pay off the men we hired and we're in the easy life for the rest of our days.

"Yes, but back there at Short Creek one man died and another one was wounded badly. Don't you care about these men that we hire, Wilbur?"

"Care? We hired men to use their guns for us. That's their life. That's why they earn five dollars a day, taking chances, risking getting killed. Hell, they wouldn't do anything else. Damnit, Barnes, just try to be a little tougher here. Think about the Smith and Barnes Machine-gun Company. That should be enough so you can stomach anything we have to do to make it happen. Things might get a lot rougher than they've been."

Canyon knew he should kill both of them right then, but he still had some rules, some ethics. He didn't gun down men from ambush without giving them a chance—

unless they were trying to kill him as the bushwacker had tried only hours before at his camp.

Besides, there were the gunman crew these men had hired who would come up shooting to defend their jobs. At least now he had a firm track on the gunmen who had attacked them back at Short Creek. They hadn't been a casual gang at all. They were hired gunslingers. Which made matters worse.

The Germans, and Smith and Barnes. Two gangs to worry about. Canyon wanted to move in closer and see where the gunmen were and how many there were. They had lost one, maybe two at Short Creek, but Smith could have hired a half-dozen more by now. Eight-to-one were not the kind of odds Canyon liked. He edged closer and then came to a halt. The clearing was just that, a natural opening in the brush where nothing but some grass grew. It might have been something in the soil. He could see three or four blanket rolls around the fire, but there could be five or six more in the edges of the brush.

Slowly, cautiously, and without making a sound, Canyon did a retrograde movement, a simple retreat out of the danger zone. When he got back to the horses, he stared for a moment into the muzzle of a six-gun.

"Easy," he said softly, and she recognized his voice. They rode again.

"Too much company on this trail," he told her after they were well away from the woods and riding north again. "How come everyone is out here trying to find your pa and we're the only ones who don't know where he's heading?"

"You said he probably was heading for the next town to go see another gunsmith."

"That was a bald-faced guess. You may have noticed that guesses often are wrong."

"Often isn't always. Where's the next town?"

"Never been in this part of the backwoods before, have you?"

"Not that I remember. How about a small hill where we can look ahead and watch for some lights?"

"Dandy idea, but the hills around here are all of six or eight feet high."

"So we ride." She looked over at him in the moonlight. Her horse moved in and their knees touched. "O'Grady, I shouldn't be telling you this, but back there when you were showing me the North Star . . ."

Canyon watched her, almost said something bright and witty, but he held it inside. This seemed to be a moment that was important for her.

"That North Star and the kisses. Just wanted to say that I kind of like that." She hurried on. "Now, don't go and get any fancy ideas. I know you like big women with bucket-sized breasts, and I've seen you buck-ass-naked right in the act. So just don't think I'm an easy woman like Betty Jo."

"I guarantee that I won't get any fancy ideas. Just remember about Betty Jo. I didn't pick her, she just dropped into my bed. About the North Star, I can say that I kind of liked that a little bit myself. Maybe I can show you the time again some night."

"You might try that, cowboy, and see. Yes, you might just try that."

They rode over the gently rolling country for another three hours, then watered their mounts at a small stream and found a campsite.

"No fire, just a few hours of sleep. A few minutes ago I smelled what must be several late-night fires. Has all the marks of a town upwind somewhere. We should find it tomorrow."

She stretched out in her blankets with all her clothes on, didn't even take off her boots. Then she sat up. "What time is it, O'Grady?"

He knelt beside her blankets, put his hands on her shoulders, and pulled her toward him gently. Then she was in his arms, her own around him tightly, her lips touching his softly at first, then harder.

He could feel her breasts crushed against his chest. He nibbled at her lips, kissed her again, and then gently pushed her away.

"It's around four o'clock somewhere and time for us to get some sleep."

"Oh, yes, now some sleep," she said, smiling in the faint moonlight that filtered through the leaves.

"Did you?" he asked.

"Did I what?"

"Did you like that?"

"Kind of," she said, smiling.

"Me too, kind of," Canyon said.

They both went to sleep at once.

A killdeer's screech brought him upright four hours later. Canyon rubbed his eyes, listened to a woodpecker banging his bill into a hollow tree somewhere, and then saw a Baltimore oriole winging from one tree to another.

'Morning, he told himself. "Hey, Merchant, it's morning. Today we're going to find that town."

The first thing he did was check her leg wound. It was starting to heal with no problems. He washed it off again with the mix from his vinegar tonic bottle and she pulled up her pants, blushing just a little, but not as much as before.

6

Before Canyon and Elizabeth rode out of the blush of brush and trees, they stopped and surveyed the land ahead. Western Missouri, the start of the great American prairie, lay before them, rolling rises but mostly flat, flat land.

A half-mile to the west they saw a pair of horsemen riding south. Canyon had no idea if they were the German pair who had attacked them last night and received a full measure of response.

The rest of the way around the horizon they could see no one and nothing.

"Let's try it," Canyon said, and they left the brush and headed north again.

Canyon left Elizabeth a few minutes to scout an east-west trail and worked a mile each way, but nowhere could he come up with the sign of the three sets of hoofprints they had followed out of Nevada.

Back at where he had left Elizabeth, he signaled and they moved out north again.

"Must be a town around here somewhere. We must be twenty miles from Nevada by now."

They rode until noon and found no sign of life, not even a farm or a three-horse ranch.

Elizabeth made them sandwiches from the last of the bread she had brought, and they rested under some linden trees along a small creek. It was shady, cool, and pleasant.

They sat near each other throwing stones in the water.

"Will we ever find my pa?" Elizabeth asked softly.

He looked at her and saw the wetness in her eyes. Gently he reached over and kissed away the tear. "We'll find him, and it will all work out, just wait and see."

"I hope so," she said. She caught his face with her hands and brought it slowly toward her, then kissed his lips. She moved and kissed his eyes closed and then kissed him again.

Slowly her mouth opened and her tongue came out, exploring. She murmured in her throat and sighed and then invited his tongue into her mouth.

"Oh, my," she said softly. "Oh, my!"

Canyon bent and kissed her again, then put one hand gently on her breast. Her eyes snapped open at his touch, then they drifted closed as he caressed her mound softly. Her mouth was open now and a moan seeped from her throat.

Her hand came up and opened two buttons on her blouse. A moment later his hand worked through the opening and slid under the chemise and captured a bare breast.

"Oh, glory," she whispered, not breaking the kiss. His hand caressed the breast, worked up to the heating nipple that rose up hard and straight.

His hand fondled her more now, moving to the other breast as he slowly eased her backward to the grass. Canyon lay partly on top of her, his hand still on her bare bosom.

She broke off the kiss. "Canyon, you know I never have before, don't you? All my talk was just talk."

She pushed upward at him and he sat up, leaving his hand on her warm breast. She caught his wrist and pulled his hand free.

"Not here," she said softly. "Not here. I've dreamed about how it would be. A real bed and a soft mattress

67

and fluffy pillows and something good to eat and drink, maybe even music . . .''

She reached over and kissed his cheek. "Maybe not all of that, but now there are two things I want: First I want to find my pa, and second, I want to see you all bare and naked again and eager to see me the same way.''

Elizabeth stood. "I'm not just teasing you, Canyon O'Grady. Maybe tonight, or tomorrow night. You understand?''

"Yes, I understand. I really thought . . .'' He stopped. "Maybe tonight.'' He stood. "Now, one more cool drink, then we'll ride.''

They made a little better time that afternoon. About four o'clock they at last found a small rise and from it they located a settlement, a town of sorts. It was a couple of miles to the east and slightly north of them.

"I can smell smoke now,'' Canyon said. "Six or eight wood stoves burning ten or twelve kinds of fire wood always makes a mess out of my nose.''

They rode into town just before five that evening. It was a string bean of a place, with a dozen stores clustered along the main street and twenty or thirty houses in back of those. It looked to be a service area for the people who lived to the east and north.

The second business they saw was the Plainsman Inn, what passed for a hotel in the town that called itself Plainsview.

Canyon looked at Elizabeth. "How about a good dinner and then a soft bed in a real inn?''

"Sounds just about perfect.''

Inside, they registered in separate rooms, and the woman who took their dollar each stared at the names a minute, then shrugged and gave them each key.

"Is there a gunsmith in town?'' Canyon asked.

The woman lifted heavy brows, ran a finger across her nose to clear away a drip, and shook her head. "Not

68

a chance. Maybe in Elroy, ten miles due east. You got a piece that don't work?''

"No, ma'am, but I'm looking for a whole new barrel.''

"Not a hope in this town.''

They went up to their rooms. They were next door to each other on the second and top floor. A sign on the inside of the door said that meals were served in the dining room. Supper was four to seven o'clock.

He put her small carpetbag in her room and watched Elizabeth sit on the bed and bounce. Then she stood quickly, a touch of embarrassment clouding her face.

"We can wash up and then have supper downstairs,'' he said. "They won't even mind our trail clothes.''

Elizabeth recovered quickly, nodded, and he went into his room. He washed off some of the trail dust, combed his red hair until it went almost where he wanted it, and then scraped off three days of beard in the cold water. He splashed some bay rum and rosewater on his face, accepting the stinging. Then he went next door and knocked on the panel.

Elizabeth opened the door and smiled. She had brushed her long blond hair until it shone, scrubbed her face, and put on a clean blouse, pink with small red roses on it. "I'm so starved that I could eat a barn,'' she said.

He chuckled. "Maybe a barn owl, that would be better than a barn swallow or a barn mouse.''

Downstairs the meal was served family-style, serve yourself from pots on the stove. Tonight the menu was beef stew, corn bread and honey, green peas and sliced tomatoes the woman must have picked out of her garden that afternoon. Plenty of coffee, thick-cut slices of bread and wild-plum jam and apple butter with just the right amount of cinnamon and clove in it.

Canyon went back to the stove for seconds and had his third cup of coffee.

Elizabeth had eaten her fill from her one large plateful and watched him with undisguised delight.

Price for the meal was fifty cents each. He gave the woman at the front desk the two-dollar gold piece and she gave him back a greenback. He hesitated before he took it.

"Green money good as gold around here, young feller," she said, and turned away.

They went upstairs and he caught Elizabeth's hand on the steps. She looked at him quickly and then smiled.

"Yes, yes, I think this is going to be a wonderful evening."

He glanced over at her, not catching the low words she had spoken. She had been watching him.

"What was that, pretty lass?"

"I was talking to myself. I do that sometimes when I'm happy and pleased and well-fed. I said I think this is going to be a wonderful evening."

He opened her door with the key and went inside with her. As soon as the door closed, he caught her in his arms and kissed her tenderly, then kissed one of her eyes, then his mouth touched hers again, hard and demanding, and she clutched at him in a sudden, exploding need.

With their mouths still together, he picked her up easily and carried her to the bed. He lay her down on her back and broke off the kiss and looked down at her.

"Young lady, Elizabeth Merchant, by name—you are sure that you want to do this? It's not too late to say good night and have a long sleep."

Her arms reached up and caught his neck and pulled him down until his face was buried in her breasts.

"Darling Canyon O'Grady, it was too late for me the first time I saw you standing outside my little house in Short Creek. I've loved you forever." She moved aside a little on the bed. "Now lay beside me before I burst."

He pulled off his boots and lay next to her.

She caught one of his hands and put it on the pink blouse. "That feels good, just having your hand there."

He reached over and kissed her. Elizabeth's eyes closed. She sighed and pushed her breasts up at his hand until he caught one and rubbed it gently. He could feel her body getting warmer, the heat radiating from her like a stove. She rolled half toward him, her foot rubbing his leg.

Slowly he unbuttoned her blouse. She nodded.

"Faster," she said, and laughed softly. "You don't know how long I've waited, how long it's been since I wanted someone to touch me there . . . and everywhere."

His hand went past the open blouse and under her white chemise.

"Oh, yes," she whispered as he touched her breast, then caressed it, heating up her soft white flesh until it nearly burned his fingers. He moved to the other breast and it warmed and the nipple enlarged and hardened.

"Oh, sweet love, I don't see how I could possibly feel any better than this."

He lifted her to a sitting position and easily took off her blouse, then lifted the chemise off over her head. Her breasts jiggled and bounced from the motion. They were large, milk-white, with big areolae of soft pink and redder nipples blooming on the tips.

"Beautiful," Canyon said. He went to his knees beside the bed and reached up and kissed her pink orbs. Elizabeth gasped. He kissed around and around and chewed on it. At last he sucked half of that breast into his mouth.

"Oh, God," she whimpered. Her arms came around his head and shoulders, pinning him to her breast as she gasped and shook, her hips pumping and her whole form vibrating in a spasm that shook her.

One climax tore through her, and before she eased down from it, another one hit her and she wailed in

71

delight. At last she pulled him with her and lay back on the bed, where she climaxed again.

She fought to get enough air into her lungs when it ended, and she leaned up on her elbows watching him come off her breast. "Good Lord, I never even dreamed anything could be that marvelous. Just fantastic."

"Elizabeth, we're just getting started. You're warming up to the really good part that comes later."

Her eyes widened and she gasped. "I think I'll die happy then, right in the middle of it."

She wanted to undress him, then. She sat up and pulled off his shirt and played with his red chest hair, giggling like a schoolgirl. Then she opened his belt and his fly.

"I've always wanted to do that, take a man's pants down. This is the very first time." She pulled his pants off and stared at the tented upthrust of his underwear.

Her eyes sparkled as she knelt at his waist, her breasts hanging down delightfully as she stripped down his underwear and let his full erection swing up. She stopped.

"My . . . I don't believe it. How can anything so big and so long go in . . ." She hid her face for a moment. "I mean . . ."

"It will, wait and see. That's something to be waiting for, looking forward to." He reached for her pants and she helped him unbutton the side and pull them down. She had on soft, loose drawers that came to her knees. When he touched them, she rolled away.

"Let's wait a minute on those," she said. "I want to look at you."

She sat beside him as he touched her breasts again. She moved closer and stared at his crotch.

"Just gets that way when you want to . . . when you get ready to . . ."

"Yes. When I see a beautiful lady and she takes her blouse off and I get to play with her pair of beautiful breasts."

"So it's not that way all the time?" She giggled.
"No, I guess not, or it would be hard to ride a horse."

He took her hand and put it on his penis. She explored, she investigated. Then he urged her on her hands and knees and lay under her. Slowly she lowered each breast into his mouth for his ministrations.

Canyon turned her on her back and kissed down her chin across her breasts to her flat little belly, and she purred. When he came to her drawers, he moved them down an inch at a time, lathering kisses as he went.

When he came to her soft blond fur, she held his head a moment. He kissed her fingertips and she let go of him. A moment later he kissed into her furry triangle and then pulled the drawers off over her feet.

Her brows went up as he lay beside her again, stretched out, pushing gently against her.

"My God, here I am in bed with a naked man," she said softly. She kissed him. "And I love it!"

His hand petted her breasts, then worked down to her stomach and down one leg.

Elizabeth shivered. His hand came up the inside of her thigh slowly. Her legs were glued together. Gently he pressed between them.

"Elizabeth, now is the time to relax. For years you've heard, Keep your knees together, don't let anyone touch. Now that's over—now, right now is the time to relax and let your knees come apart and relax again and enjoy."

"I know, but it's hard."

"I won't do anything you don't want me to do, all right?"

She frowned a moment, then grinned and kissed him. "Fine, yes, all right."

His hand went between her knees again and he pushed then and they parted. He kissed her, then slowly worked his hand up the inside of her thigh. She was breathing fast and heavily again.

Once more he came toward her crotch and this time

she held her breath. Gently with a soft touch, his fingers fluttered over her swollen, wet lips.

"Oh! Oh! Yes, that is fine. It feels so . . . so wonderful."

He did the same thing again, a bit firmer this time. She responded the same way. He caught her hand and put it to his erection and she held on.

This time when his fingers touched her, he moved higher until he found the small hard node and he stroked it, making her jump.

"Oh, God, you know about that, too?"

"The best part," he whispered in her ear, his fingers dancing. Magical moments later, Elizabeth moaned and was lost into another climax harder and stronger than the times before. She surged up and hugged Canyon pulling his face into her breasts.

"Oh, glory. I didn't think anything could be so wonderful."

It was getting dark in the room. He got up and lit the one lamp in the room and turned up the wick. There was no blind on the window, but they were on the second floor and no one could look inside except from a long distance.

He lay back down on his side.

"Good! He's still here and still solid."

"Your job is to turn him into a soft worm, eventually."

"What?"

"You'll see." He kissed her and put his hand back to her crotch and stroked her nether lips, finding them warm and wet. With one finger he entered her an inch, and she grinned.

"Yes, yes, I'm ready. I want to see how you're gonna do this. He's just too big."

Canyon spread her knees and pushed between them, then put some saliva in his hand and coated the purple tip of his weapon. He looked at her. "You're sure?"

She nodded and held her breath.

"Then, relax. It's natural and normal."

Canyon eased into the slot, waited a minute, and then gently worked in and out, going a little deeper each time. A minute later he was fully inserted and their pelvic bones touched.

"That's as far as it goes," Canyon said, kissing her lips.

"My God, I'm getting fucked," Elizabeth crooned.

He eased in and out a few time, then established a rhythm of stroking. Soon her little bottom came up to meet him on each stroke.

"Now that is fine," he said.

"Absolutely wildly fantastic," she whispered.

She was built low and he could feel on each stroke that he was touching her clit. Now it was a race to see who would erupt first. He pounded faster and faster. She humped against him and sweat broke out on her forehead. Her legs had lifted and now wound around his back and locked together.

They bucked and drove and responded and ground together.

"I'm going to do it again," she screeched.

Then Canyon couldn't speak. He was surging up the mountain. He was almost over the top when she jolted into another spasm; that set him off and for ten seconds it was a thrashing, pounding, grunting, and wailing contest. Then he erupted inside her and she felt the hot fluids and drove through another climax. They both fell in a heap on the bed, panting and sweating and body parts still jolting and responding.

Neither of them made another sound for ten minutes. He lay heavily on her, but she didn't complain. Then she opened one eye to see if his eyes were open. They were.

"I may never leave this bed. What a marvelous, wonderful, exciting experience!" She breathed heavily for a minute. "God, I'll never be the same again! I'll probably try to go to bed with every man I find."

"You'll feel differently about that in an hour or so. Not entirely different. You'll see."

"Let's do it again, right now!"

He pulled away from her and sat on the side of the bed and she moaned at the loss of him.

"That's not nice."

He chuckled. "Remember I was telling you it was your job to turn me into a worm. Look."

She stared at his limpness for a moment and then laughed. "I guess I did. Make him big and strong again."

"That's a part you don't know about. A woman can climax all day long. With a man, he needs some recuperation time."

"Well, we have all night."

They did have all night. They lasted for three times, then both were simply too sleepy to function again. They held each other and went to sleep.

Morning came slowly, and Canyon lay there wide awake since five watching it get light. When dawn was full, he slid out of bed and dressed quickly. He heard something and looked down to see Elizabeth awake and watching him.

"Never seen a man dress before," she said. "Interesting."

"Now it's my turn to watch you dress. I want an early start this morning. When do they serve breakfast?"

He saw it on the sign on the door. "From six A.M. to eight A.M.," he said. Then he sat on the wooden chair and watched her dress.

They had breakfast—flapjacks and butter and syrup, eggs over easy, bacon and grits, toast and jam, and coffee.

After they ate, Canyon went out to the front desk and found the same woman there wearing the same blue dress.

"If your pa came this way, chances are he'd stay at a hotel or such," he told Elizabeth.

The woman behind the small counter watched them, and when he looked at her, she responded. "Yes, sir, breakfast all right?"

"Good, extremely good. I have a question. I'm looking for a traveling man. Name of Hirum Merchant. Did he by any chance stay here within the past three or four days."

The woman didn't need to look at the register. She nodded. "Indeed he did. Fact is he stayed two nights. Met an Englishman here and they talked. Then two days ago he left us with his horse and packhorse. He and Mr. Vickers were going to travel together. They asked me where an out-of-the-way place was where they could do some target-shooting. I sent them up toward Willow Gap. No people around there for miles."

"You say they went there two days ago?"

" 'Deed I did. Mr. Merchant was telling Mr. Vickers he had a day or so of work on something before he'd be ready to demonstrate. Whatever that means."

"This is important. Could you tell me exactly how to get to Willow Gap? We have to go up there. I'm afraid Mr. Merchant is in extreme danger."

7

Canyon pushed the pace as fast as he could. Elizabeth had taken the news about her father well. Now she sat on the small bay and rode with a grim determination. Her mouth was set in that do-or-die way she had, and her eyes were flinty and full of purpose. Nothing was going to stop her now from finding and saving her father.

Willow Gap was a ten-mile ride from what the innkeeper had said. It gave Canyon a lot of time to think. She had said Hirum told the Englishman that he needed another day to work on the project before he was ready to demonstrate it.

Good. Canyon hoped Hirum had run into more problems. If the gun was working perfectly, the Englishman had only to kill Merchant and take the weapon as his own. The British military would make him a general, the queen would knight him, and he would be rich for the rest of his life.

"How much farther?" Elizabeth asked.

He hadn't been thinking about the distance. "Another five miles. Another hour."

The landscape had changed. Now they were in a section of small hills, riding down a valley that was little more than a canyon. There had been no signs, but the landmarks had been well described and Canyon had found them and followed the trail easily.

What would happen when he found the two men? He hoped there would still be two men. He'd play that scene out when he got there. Elizabeth would be somewhere in the backround if he could manage it. Keeping her alive and safe was now one of his major projects.

Canyon picked up the pace again, sending the mounts in a trot for a half-mile, then eased back to a steady walk. The track now wound higher in the little canyon. Hills stretched above them on each side. The slopes were covered with lots of oak and ash here, with an American elm now and again. He saw redbud and persimmon and even a few papaw trees.

Grimly he pushed on, afraid of what he would find. The Englishman would probably be gone and Hirum Merchant's bullet-riddled body would be sprawled in the dirt beside a pile of brass shell casings from the test firing.

The vision made Canyon urge the horses along faster. For the fourth or fifth time he checked the Spencer to be sure there was a round in the chamber. He'd have eight shots that way. His six-gun was primed and ready. It was a risk having one round under the hammer, but this was the time to take such a chance.

The land slanted up again, and ahead he could see where there was a gap in the hills. This must be Willow Gap, but he couldn't see a single willow tree. The brush and trees were thick here, and as the canyon blended in with the flatter area near the top of the low hills, he knew they were about there.

The single rifle shot jolted him as he heard it in the clear morning air. The round did not come near them, but he ducked automatically.

Elizabeth looked up. She trembled, then frowned as if catching hold tightly on her emotions. "Where?"

"Ahead," Canyon said. "Up there past the trees. When we get closer, we'll find out what's happening. If there's any shooting at us, I'll want you well away from it. You must do as I say here or you could get yourself killed. Do you understand?"

"Yes, unless I can help."

"I may have to tie you up."

She glowered at him. "You wouldn't do that, Canyon O'Grady."

He let it lay there and rode faster.

Two minutes later they came to a spot where the brush and trees stopped. The land ahead was layered with sheets of rocks and almost no topsoil so no trees could grow. Here and there a stunted oak struggled to survive, but they were not over three feet tall.

Most of the area was covered with grass and a few taller weeds.

About twenty yards from the woods were two men bending over a device anchored to the ground with a tripod arrangement. To one side stood six men with rifles. The voices came clearly over the short distance.

"You don't seem to understand, Mr. Merchant, exactly what has happened here. I am in control. I have six gunmen who will gladly shoot you down in an instant if I tell them to. What I want from you is a demonstration that the weapon will shoot more than one round at a time."

"I showed you, it worked," Merchant said. He was a foot shorter than the towering Englishman, slight, and seemed to be wearing spectacles.

"I'm starting to lose my patience with you, Merchant. Right now I want you to put in the belt filled with shells and show me how it will fire fully automatic. Then, and only then, will I be satisfied."

They saw Merchant working over the side of the gun. He lifted a canvas belt evidently filled with rounds and put it through a section of the gun. He pulled back a black handle and Canyon could hear a round being chambered.

"Stand back," Merchant said. "I've only done this a few times and I can't guarantee it will work."

Vickers backed up two steps and watched closely.

Merchant squatted behind the weapon, pointed it

across the clearing a hundred yards at a cardboard box he had set up, and pulled the trigger.

A stuttering sound came and Canyon counted five separate shots. There was a pause, then the gun chattered again with a ten-round burst of deadly fire.

The Englishman shouted for joy. He threw a small cane in the air, lifted Hirum Merchant up from in back of the gun, and hugged him.

"By Jove, you've done it! A fully automatic weapon. You'll be famous and rich. I have made out a bill of sale. I will personally pay you a thousand pounds, that's over five thousand U.S. dollars. Then you will receive a production royalty on each gun manufactured of six dollars. You'll be an extremely rich man. Every nation in the world will want this weapon and they'll have to come to me to get it. I can charge them any price I want to."

"One small problem, Mr. Vickers," Merchant said. He took off his glasses and polished them on a white handkerchief. "I tell you again, the gun is not for sale. I will not sell it to you or to anyone. The United States government has first claim on its use. I doubt very much that they will want me to sell any to other nations."

"Ridiculous, Merchant. We have discussed that. I will raise my price to three thousand pounds and eight dollars a gun. You will have the chance to come to England to help set up the manufacturing of the guns." Vickers went on as if the matter was settled. "Now, you said there was one more problem with the gun. It overheats."

"Yes, but I'm designing a water jacket to go around the twenty-six-inch barrel. The water will cool the barrel so it can fire two hundred rounds a minute for extended periods of time. That will take me only a day or two, once I get to a good machine shop." He scowled. "But that's of no concern to you, Mr. Vickers, because I am not selling you this weapon."

"Is that your final word, Mr. Merchant?"

"It was final two days ago, Mr. Vickers. Now, I'm packing up here and moving back toward Kansas City, where I have friends who will help me with fabricating the water jacket."

"Oh, you're going to move, all right, Mr. Merchant. But not to Kansas City. You're coming east with us to the Mississippi. Then we'll go downstream to the first British ship we can find, and two weeks later we all will be in England with my new invention. As my loyal and trusted assistant, you will be brought along."

"I'm not selling—"

"That's exactly right, Merchant. You refused to sell, so I'm simply taking the weapon from you, kidnapping you as long as I need you, and then disposing of your worthless carcass in the river. Now do you understand?"

Canyon and Elizabeth huddled in the brush twenty yards away, watching.

She gripped his arm. "We have to do something," she whispered.

"Not now. Not against seven guns. We'll stay out of sight and see what happens."

Vickers called two of his gunmen. They came and held Merchant as Vickers knelt behind the weapon and looked at it. Then he put his finger on the trigger under the oblong black box and triggered the weapon.

He held it back for six rounds, laughed with delight, and then fired ten more, then five again. The stuttering rounds tore into the area around the box on the far slope. Vickers touched the barrel of the weapon and pulled his finger away quickly.

"You're right about the cooling. We have to keep the barrel cool or it will twist and warp and be worthless." He motioned to the men. "Bring the horses out and let's pack up this gear and be on our way. We can get a good day's travel in before nightfall. I've already checked. This gap extends down the other side to a road that soon leads east. Look sharp now and let's break our camp and get moving.''

Canyon caught Elizabeth's hand and they led their horses back into the denser undergrowth past large clumps of blackberry vines and hackberry.

"We can't just let them ride away," Elizabeth snarled at Canyon.

"That's precisely what we're going to do. We can't go up against seven guns out there. It's three or four days to the Mississippi. As soon as they make their camp tonight, we'll move in on them. I'm certain they will camp outdoors. They can't risk letting anyone see you father and track him.''

"But they might hurt him.''

"Not right now. He's safe as a newborn babe in his mother's arms. They still need your father to finish the design and then to show them how to manufacture the gun. He's safe enough.''

"You're sure?''

"Absolutely. It's what I would do if I were stealing your father's invention. What we have to do now is stay out of sight until tonight, then surprise them, rescue your father and his weapon, and charge away to the nearest U.S. Army fort or camp, where your father will have protection.''

She watched him from pale-green eyes that now seemed as large as a new moon. Her face worked a minute. "I want to believe you. But if I do, and you're wrong, and they . . . If something bad happens to Pa, I'll blame myself.''

"Do you think you and I could attack those seven men out there and beat them? We'd have to kill them all, or capture them.''

She sighed and he liked what it did to her full breasts as they rose and surged and then fell. She shook her head. "No, I guess you're right. We couldn't beat them. We'll have to wait.''

"Night and sleep will be our two biggest helpers. It's almost noon. In seven hours it will be dark and we'll figure out how to rescue your pa."

That seemed to satisfy her. They watched as the men brought in horses that were ready for the trail. Merchant took the gun itself off the tripod and lashed it on a packhorse. The tripod arrangement folded and was tied on the other side. The rest of the goods in long cardboard boxes were lashed to the packhorse. There was some talk by Vickers about tying Hirum to his horse, but he said that wouldn't be necessary. The little caravan moved out straight ahead over the end of the pass and down the other side.

Canyon waited for half an hour after they were out of sight, then he and Elizabeth worked their mounts slowly around the edge of the clearing but just inside the brush to be out of sight. At the edge of the pass they came into the open and looked out and could see the nine horses working down another narrow valley a half-mile below them.

"Good," Canyon said. "Now all we have to do is follow them."

"And hope that the Germans or those American gun-makers haven't found the inn yet," Elizabeth said. "I wonder where they are?"

As if in answer to her question, a rifle shot sounded behind them and a bullet whipped over their heads. Both surged their horses into the brush and out of sight before the gunman could fire again.

Canyon took his Spencer and edged up to the clearing. He could see two horsemen near the far side of the rocky opening that led up the way they had come that morning. Both men were riding forward at a gallop. They were two hundred yards away.

"Deadly force given means deadly force returned," Canyon said softly. He sighted in with the Spencer and tracked the first horseman. When the sight firmed on the man's chest, Canyon squeezed the trigger. The first round took the rider out of the saddle with a gut shot; the man screamed and pivoted off the horse, slamming to the ground and rolling over and over. His horse kept coming forward.

The second rider hesitated.

Canyon levered a fresh round into the Spencer and fired again, then again. The third shot hit the horse in the chest and it reared in pain and anger. The rider fell off and the horse reversed direction and ran hard for the downhill trail it had just come up.

Canyon watched for the man. He rolled over and came up with a six-gun and fired, but he was three times out of range. The man lunged ahead, then turned and raced for the underbrush. Canyon fired off his last three shots before the runner made it to the brush.

He got up and hurried back to where Elizabeth held the horses.

"One is down, the other one in the brush. I have to go get him or he could ruin everything. Stay here with the horses and keep that six-gun of yours handy."

He ran forward through the light growth toward where the man had entered the brush. He went fifty yards, then stopped still and listened. He heard nothing moving ahead of him. The man had come off his horse about a hundred yards ahead of Canyon. He had to be close.

Canyon worked slowly forward now, eyes alert, watching every bush, every tree. He leaned against a tall hickory and looked around it.

Nothing.

He listened again, then crept forward, not putting down his foot until he was sure nothing under it would snap or break. He moved another twenty feet. For a moment he thought he heard something ahead. Canyon paused, sniffing the air, but he could not be sure what was ahead of him. Something moved again.

Canyon lifted his six-gun in his right hand and worked through some brush as he moved forward. Three steps, four, then two more. The sound came again, a rustling of leaves of the mulch on the woods floor.

He parted leaves of a bush and saw something. Then a big jackrabbit stood up on its hind legs, nose quivering, huge ears pointing Canyon's direction. The jack caught the man scent and scurried off into the brush.

Canyon lifted his brows and listened again. There was nothing, no movement, no noise.

A wailing scream pierced through the air. It was Elizabeth behind him. He heard her gun fire and then a man swearing.

Canyon swore himself, reversed himself, and rushed back toward the horses. He made no attempt to keep quiet this time. He wanted the man to hear him. He crashed brush and then stopped quickly behind a tree just when he could see the horses.

"I've got you covered," he called out. "No way you can get away alive. Toss down your weapon and stand up."

"He's German," Elizabeth cried. "He doesn't understand English."

Canyon began working ahead slowly. They should be tracking Hirum and the Englishman, not wasting time with the damn Germans. He edged forward with the six-gun, parting bushes and grass as he crawled. The German would be looking high. He'd come in low and surprise the bastard.

Another six feet he crawled. Now he could see both horses, but where was Elizabeth and the German?

Canyon used an old trick, but one that works almost every time with a nervous gunman. His hand closed around a good-sized rock and he threw it to the side, away from the horses. The rock hit, crashing through a dead branch and careening off a tree trunk, making a lot of noise.

Almost at once a weapon blasted a shot. The pall of blue smoke from the powder showed to the right of the horses. Closer to him. Canyon moved that way softly.

He stayed low. There was no more response from Elizabeth. One of the German's hands must be over her mouth: That left him only one hand. Good.

Canyon moved agonizingly slowly, a crawling, cautious motion, to work under the brush and near the tree trunks. Ahead he saw a swatch of pink. Elizabeth's blouse. He rubbed his eyes and looked again. Just to the left of the blouse he saw a blue shirt. On the shirt was a large red stain that was growing.

Canyon edged closer until he could see the German's head. His eyes were closed. He snapped them open and looked toward where the rock had hit. He tried to lift the six-gun he carried, but it came up, then sagged downward.

Canyon checked the brush the ten feet between them. There were no big trees or shrubs between them. The man held Elizabeth around the neck with one arm. Canyon holstered his six-gun and snapped the hold-down strap, then bunched his legs under him, getting ready.

He exploded out of the brush with a roar, drove three steps forward, and then dived at the man holding Elizabeth. The six-gun came up, then the man screamed in pain as Elizabeth bit hard into his arm, drawing blood.

The German dropped the gun about the time Canyon hit him in the jaw with his extended right fist. The man rolled away from Elizabeth, the gun gone, and he lay on his back.

Canyon grabbed his throat with both hands until there was no breath left in the man. Then he looked at Elizabeth. "You all right?"

"Close to it," she said, rubbing her neck.

Canyon looked back at the German. He was the big one who could speak English. "He's dead?" Elizabeth asked.

"Yes. It was his fault, not yours."

She leaned over to him and cried. He held her and kissed her neck and patted her back. It took her five minutes to get the cry all out of her system.

"I've never killed a human being before," she said, drying her eyes. "I had no idea it would hurt this bad. I never want to feel this way again."

Canyon stood. "Don't think about it. He would have gladly killed you to get the gun. High time we get away from here. We have to catch up with your pa. He's the one in this little game who is the important one."

They rode through the pass and down the other side, tracking the eight horses and the deadly machine gun. They were too close now to let the Englishman get away with the prize.

8

Canyon O'Grady and his small shadow, Elizabeth, worked down the grade from Willow Gap, riding faster as the land leveled out again. Soon the tracks of the nine horses swung to the east through open fields, near a scattering of farms and ranches.

They did not stop to rest their horses or for a midday meal.

Canyon worried that they were making better time than he had guessed they might. His estimate of three days' ride to the Mississippi was far short, he now realized. The state of Missouri was two hundred fifty miles wide and they would have to cover most of it to get to the Mississippi River.

At thirty miles a day it would still take them eight days to make the trip. No wonder Vickers was pushing his men. Canyon knew he could catch them alone. With Elizabeth it would be harder.

He looked over at her. "Hey, soldier, how are you doing?"

"I am fine." She said the words with measured assurance, which made him suspicious.

"I'm sorry, but we have to keep going. This bunch is making good time. Our best hope is that they will quit early today and we can run them down tonight. It's going to mean a long day, and a few saddle sores or a sore bottom at least."

Elizabeth laughed with good humor. "Sore? Let me tell you about sore, big tough man. I'm sore right now in a place I never even knew a girl could get sore. 'Stretched' maybe is the word.'' She grinned at him. ''But it's the best kind of hurt I've ever had. I wouldn't trade it for a million dollars.''

''Good. We'll ride for another two hours, then rest the horses for twenty minutes and let them graze and water. Then be gone again. We can't lose your pa now.''

''Right. Don't worry about me. You set the pace and I'll keep up if I have to get off and run.''

Canyon grinned back at her. He was starting to like this girl more than he should. Last night didn't help any. This was just part of his job. She didn't mean a thing to him. She couldn't. He was footloose, all over the whole United States and its territories and free land. But even as he thought it through, he knew he didn't really believe that she was just another romp in the bedroom.

They watered the mounts near a small creek that merged with another larger river. The Osage was around here somewhere and the cluster of lakes. They had to catch Vickers sometime tonight. Only, how was he going to track them once the sun went down? Canyon had done some tracking by lantern, establishing a direction, riding a quarter of a mile, and checking for tracks again with the lantern, but he couldn't do that in this moist, hilly country they were coming to.

About four that afternoon they found where the Englishman and his men had stopped, started a fire, and cooked a meal. The horse droppings were still warm, but the fire had gone cold.

''Three hours ahead of us,'' Canyon said. ''Which means we have to strike out faster. We'll use a gallop-and-walk pattern and see how long our horses can hold out.''

They went back on the trail. It followed a stream now that angled almost due east. Canyon put his big bay into a gallop for a quarter of a mile, then walked her briskly for a half-mile to cool her out, made sure of the trail, and galloped for another quarter of a mile.

The bay reacted well to it, but the smaller roan tired after the third gallop. This time he walked the mounts for a full mile before he galloped again.

Once he galloped right past a turn in the trail and lost fifteen minutes finding where the Vickers group had cut across the stream at a shallow spot and kept on their eastward trek.

Smoke. He would have to find them tonight by his nose. They would surely start a fire. There would be little to suggest that anyone was on their trail. The shots on the pass after they had left could have been from anyone, even from hunters. There should be deer in that hilly country, and maybe a black bear or two.

Canyon stopped at the top of a small hill and stared ahead. He couldn't see any movement, not even antlike figures pacing along two or three miles ahead of them. Neither did he find many farms or ranches.

He moved up beside the girl and touched her shoulder. Then he leaned half off his mount and gave her a firm hug. She clung to him.

"Hey, don't worry. We're going to find them and get your pa back. You wait and see. Have I ever lied to you . . . lately?"

She laughed and then kissed his cheek. "Tonight, is there going to be time to be close, to come together, you know?"

"Not if we can find them. That's the big job right now. Then later there will be lots and lots of time for the two of us to get really well acquainted."

"In a soft, fluffy bed?"

"Or even beside a gurgling stream out in the open."

"Oh, I think I'd like that. Just so you're all naked and bare and loving me." She kissed his lips, then let go of him, and they pushed on.

Just before darkness settled in, Canyon stopped his bay on a slight rise and looked east. He wanted to pick out landmarks he could find in the dark or, he hoped, in the moonlight. There were no towering mountain peaks to sight in on.

It would be up to his nose. He tested the wind. Usually the prevailing breezes were west to east, which didn't help any. But at night the wind would be calmer and could swirl a little. At worst he would catch the scent of the smoke as soon as he passed their fire.

With darkness they watched ahead carefully, looking for the glow of a campfire. They saw one about an hour after sunset, but it turned out to be a small fire at a ranch house. They rode past without any contact with the rancher/farmer. They continued for another hour before they stopped.

"How can you tell we're on the right track?" Elizabeth asked.

"I can't. Half-guess, half-instinct. By the stars I know we're still heading due east. Stars are a big help that way. We'll give it another hour; then, if we don't find smoke, we'll have to wait until morning."

He knew she was smiling at him. "That might not be so bad. I'm tired and sore and wanting your arms around me."

"Soon, little flower, soon."

He stretched it to an hour and a half. Just as he was about to call a halt, the sharp smell of wood smoke came to him on an easy breeze. Behind them. They had bypassed Vickers' fire. He touched Elizabeth's shoulder and whispered to her. They moved slowly now at an angle to the trail they had just come on. He tied kerchiefs around the muzzles of the mounts, then got off and walked his horse forward.

The smoke smell became stronger. He tied his horse and leaned up and whispered to Elizabeth. "Stay here. I'm going to move up and see if this is Vickers or another farm."

She started to say something and he shook his head. "I know you want to come, but don't. This way, if anything up there moves and it's their camp, I'll know it will be an enemy. Do you understand?''

She nodded. She bent and kissed his lips and he faded into the night toward the smoke.

Canyon had a feeling about this one. He moved through the grasslands easily at a trot, then came to a copse of woods. He had not seen it in the blackness. The moon had not cooperated and he could barely see ten feet in front of him.

He worked through the brush with deliberate slowness. Patience and care were the key words here. Thirty feet into the woods he stopped and listened. The time must be before nine o'clock. Surely they wouldn't be sleeping yet.

But he heard nothing, no voices, no horses.

Canyon moved forward again, slightly faster now. It could be another false alarm. Fifty feet ahead he found a creek and he edged through the brush along the side of the stream moving to the right, and he still had the smell of wood smoke in his nostrils.

The creek took a small turn to the left and then he saw a fire. It was not a campfire, rather a bonfire. Now he saw forms moving around it. He edged closer. He counted four men. They were passing a bottle around. Was it Vickers and his hired crew of gunmen?

Canyon worked closer until he was only thirty feet from the edge of the firelight.

Yes! He spotted the Englishman sitting on a fold-out camp stool watching the men. He had them! Now all he had to do was wait until they all went to sleep. If they left a guard, that man would die. Canyon moved away from the fire now, walking quickly, knowing that their talking and the sound of the fire and the chattering stream would mask his slight noises. The horses were less than fifty yards from the fire.

He made enough noise coming so Elizabeth heard him. She lowered the handgun when she saw him.

"It's them," he whispered. "I didn't see your father,

but I'm sure he's there somewhere. They're passing a bottle, so they all should be sleeping soon."

"I'm going in with you."

"No." He kissed her lips, hard, eagerly knowing that he had to convince her. He broke away. "The same idea, I want to be free to shoot if I need to. We'll move the horses down the stream a ways and let them drink and graze. You keep them safe. I'll be back as soon as I can, and I won't come back without your pa." He watched her in the soft night air. "You understand?"

She nodded. He kissed her again.

"No fair sneaking up there, I might think you were one of them. Right now I need your ironbound and most sincere promise on this. I don't want to kill you thinking one of them is about to kill me."

Her mouth made a small "O" as if now it made sense. She reached up and kissed his lips. "Now I understand, Canyon. I'll stay here and wait. Really, I will." She kissed him again. Then she took his hand and pressed it to her breasts. "You have my word of honor."

"Good. I'll be back."

He led the horses to his right to the stream they hadn't seen yet, let them drink, then tied them where they could munch on some lush grass.

"Now, small, beautiful lady, you stay right here." He kissed her lips quickly and went along the stream at a jog until he came to the brush, then he slowed and worked into it carefully.

He found the fire as before. Now only two men were at the flames drinking. Vickers was in blankets somewhere as well. Canyon edged up closer, his six-gun in hand and ready. Habit. He put the revolver away, snapped the hold-down strap, and took out a six-inch, wide-bladed hunting knife. Quiet time.

It was a half-hour before the last man near the fire emptied the bottle of whiskey and threw it into the woods. Then he hunkered down where he was by the fire and began to snore. If he rolled over, he'd burn half his leg off.

The fire was down to glowing coals now, a pile two feet square with a lot of heat but not much light. As Canyon watched, a man walked up to the fire and bent to warm his hands.

A guard! The man walked toward where Canyon lay. Coming away from the fire, he'd be night-blind for thirty seconds. He walked straight toward Canyon. The United States agent stood silently, and when the guard was within four feet of him, Canyon drove ahead with the heavy knife held like a lance on the end of his ramrod-stiff arm.

The blade drove into the guard's chest, slated off a rib, and plunged through the man's heart. He died without a whimper, simply melted and sank to the ground.

Canyon caught the man's rifle and lay it on the ground beside him. He found a hand-sized rock and approached the first sleeping man. It took two solid thunks on the skull to be sure the man was unconscious.

Canyon tied him hand and foot with strips of rawhide and moved to the next man. He had three of them knocked out and tied up when the next one came awake and growled.

"Harry, what the hell you doing?" the man asked.

Canyon turned with the rock and hit him too hard on the side of his head. There would be no real need to tie that one. He got two more tied up, then found Hirum at the side away from the others. He was tied hand and foot.

Canyon cut the ropes that held Hirum and then woke him up, a hand over his mouth.

"Mr. Merchant," Canyon whispered, "I'm here to help you. My name is Canyon O'Grady. You're untied. I want you to come with me. Your daughter, Elizabeth, is here and wants to help you. Do you understand?''

Hirum Merchant nodded.

Canyon took his hand away from the man's mouth.

''I don't know who you are, but I'm glad to see you. I won't leave without my big gun.''

''Which horse is it on?''

''Not sure. We'll go take a look.''

They stood and Merchant stumbled a moment getting his legs working again.

''Elizabeth is really here?''

''Yes. I'm trying to help get you to a U.S. Army fort, where you can finish work on your gun and not be bothered by all these people.''

''Yes, yes. A good idea. The horses are down this way.''

They had moved only a few feet when a figure loomed in front of them.

''Now, Hirum, old man, where do you think you're going?''

Canyon pulled his six-gun and fired all in one smooth move. The bullet hit Vickers and knocked him down. Hirum ran ahead and found the horses. He picked out the horse he had been riding and cinched up the saddle girth strap, then he grabbed a lead line on the horse still loaded with the machine gun.

''Let's get out of here, boy,'' Hirum shrilled.

Canyon grabbed another horse, cinched up the saddle, and stepped into the leather. They rode downstream.

''This the right direction?'' Hirum asked.

''This is where my horse and Elizabeth are waiting,'' Canyon said.

They rode a short ways and Elizabeth called. They found her already mounted and she called out softly when she saw her father.

''Pa, I'm so glad you're safe. We been looking for you for days now. You can trust this man, Canyon

O'Grady.'' They leaned together and hugged. Then Canyon rode up. "We better get out of here. I'm not sure that I put down Vickers to stay." They reversed their direction, riding back to the west.

"Pa, that really you?" Elizabeth shouted.

"What's left of me. Don't understand why all these people are chasing me all of a sudden."

Canyon laughed. "You really don't know?"

"Not by a dang sight. Unless they want to steal my gun."

"That gun of yours will revolutionize modern warfare, Mr. Merchant. Germany, England, half the countries in the world would give their crown jewels to get their hands on that machine gun of yours. We saw it fire when you demonstrated it for Vickers."

"Not a good man, that Vickers. He had me fooled at first. Said he'd help me get back to Kansas City."

"Sounds like a good idea," Canyon said. "We'll take you there and right on through to Fort Leavenworth, twenty miles or so into Kansas. There the whole damn army will protect you and give you time to finish your gun."

"About time, young feller. I wrote the army a letter last year asking them to do just that."

"Well, Mr Merchant, you know how slow the army is to get things done." He looked behind them. Elizabeth was still leading his big bay by the reins.

"Let's stop a minute so I can change horses, then we better pick up the pace a little so we can get as big a head start as we can on Vickers. Don't know for sure if I hit him bad back there or not."

Canyon traded horses and let the borrowed one go. Then they rode northwest until they picked up a county road of some sort and stayed on that. It was probably heading due west, which was fine by Canyon. He could adjust in the morning. The road gave them a sure surface and they trotted for a while, then walked the mounts again.

"I ain't ridden a horse this much in years," Hirum said. "Thought if I kept moving I could stay ahead of them guys. Vickers has been at me before, but I figured I had him talked out of his scheme."

"Did some Germans find you?" Elizabeth asked.

"Not that I remember."

"You would have remembered these guys," Canyon said. "They come in shooting first and asking questions later. We don't have to worry about them anymore."

"What happened to them?" Hirum asked.

"They encountered severe stomach and digestive problems," Canyon said.

Hirum chuckled. "You shot them, right?"

"Something like that."

Just then they heard three gunshots fired behind them a long ways off.

"Pistol or a revolver," Hirum said. "Seems that chunk of lead of yours didn't put Vickers down for good. We'll be meeting him again tomorrow, I'd suspect."

"He still has four men," Canyon said.

Hirum watched Canyon as they rode.

"Canyon O'Grady, you said your name was. You work with the government or something?"

"Something like that. My job is to get you and your gun safely into army hands. The army only wants to give you room and board and a place to work and test your weapon. You will own all rights to its patents, and it hopes if it's successful that you'll give the United States army the exclusive rights to buy the weapon."

"Sounds damn fair, considering what our friend Vickers had in mind," Hirum said. "How much farther we got to go?"

"About a hundred miles, more or less," Canyon said.

"Let's make it in three days, I want to get back to work. I've got to get the gun finished."

"Design and build that water jacket for the barrel, right, Pa?" Elizabeth said.

"Now, how did you know that?"

"We heard you talking with the Englishman up at Willow Gap," Elizabeth said.

"Yep, that I've got to do, and a few small fine tunings on the recoil mechanism. Not all that complicated, once you get the basic idea working. What surprises me is that nobody thought of doing this before."

"Mr. Merchant, we ran into another bunch who are looking for you. Have you ever heard of some gunmakers called Smith and Barnes?"

"Lots of Smiths around who claim to be gunsmiths. Never met one who said he was a gunmaker. Knew a guy named Smith, but he was teamed up with a guy named Wesson. Couldn't be the same bunch."

"No, not the same team. These two want simply to steal your gun, kill you, and call it their own. Downright unfriendly of them, I'd say."

Hirum looked through the darkness at the big man riding beside him. "Vickers took my handgun. You wouldn't happen to have a spare, would you, Mr. O'Grady?"

"Canyon is the name, and I do carry a spare sixgun in my saddlebags. Next stop I'll get it out and load it up for you."

"Be much obliged."

They rode faster then. The moon came out from behind scudding clouds and lighted the way. They hit a larger road and let the horses gallop for a quarter of a mile, then settled them down to a quick walking pace.

"Six hundred rounds a minute?" Canyon asked, looking over at Hirum.

"Yep. That's what we call the firing rate. 'Course, that would twist up a barrel all to smithereens if you tried to fire six hundred without letting up on the trigger."

"I saw it fire ten, eleven rounds at a time," Canyon said. "It's a fantastic weapon. You know that such a gun will revolutionize warfare, don't you? Think what one army could do to another with ten or twelve of these guns covering a two-hundred-yard fighting front."

"Probably," Hirum Merchant said. "Me, I'm just a mechanic. I make the machine so it works. I don't know nothing about war or tactics or that sort of thing. I leave that up to the generals." He looked up at Canyon. "Never met a general. Suppose I can meet one when we get to Fort Leavenworth?"

Canyon grinned in the darkness. "Meet one? You'll have a dozen generals crawling over one another to shake you hand. You'll be the most popular man on the post for dances and fancy dinners. You're going to be famous and soon rich, I hope, Mr. Merchant."

"Well, land sakes. All that over one small little machine gun. Now, that is something to ponder."

9

They stopped riding about three in the morning. They all were so tired they barely could sit their horses. Canyon said they would sleep until daylight and then watch their back trail for a while. Later on, they would ride again, push on to the biggest town they could find, and rest up a day.

"No," Hirum said quickly. "I want to keep on going as fast as we can so I can get Betsy here safe in the hands of the army. Then I'll be able to sleep a little better."

They settled down in a small grove of trees, mostly hazelnut and elm, Canyon thought. The horses were left saddled and ready to ride at a moment's notice.

Elizabeth and her father had been talking nonstop since they rolled out their blankets near each other. There was a lot to catch up on.

Canyon didn't think he was that tired at first, but as soon as he sat down and pulled the blanket around him, he felt the weariness cloud his mind, pulling him apart, dropping him in a hundred places back along the trail they had ridden. He wasn't sure that three hours' sleep would be enough time for him to race back and gather up all of his body parts and paste himself back together. What if it wasn't enough time and he awoke in the daylight and several of his vital parts were not quite . . .

Canyon rolled over and sat up.

It was morning, the sun was well up. He checked the other bedrolls and they were both occupied, the owners sleeping. He thought back to his early training on how to make a smokeless fire, and he walked along the creek, trying to find enough dead driftwood left in the brush at some high-water time.

The sticks were white with age and so dry they couldn't have a thimbleful of smoke in a bushel. He gathered as many as he could carry and went back and made a small fire. He placed the black coffeepot directly over the flames. He fed in finger-sized sticks to the blaze and saw with satisfaction that there was no more than a slight tinge of smoke even ten feet over the fire. It would not be seen. A good nose might smell it if that nose was within half a mile.

The coffee boiled.

He nudged the two awake and tried to smile at them. "We need to get moving. I have a feeling that our English friend, Mr. Vickers, will be pounding the trail behind us. At least one of his four men must know something about tracking and would soon find that we were on the way north and west again."

"You're joking about us riding again," Elizabeth said. She was rumpled and only half-awake. One eye squinted at him, hiding most of the pale green. He touched her shoulder and she started to lean toward him.

Her father coughed and spit, then stood. "Damn early in the day to be getting up," he said, then wandered out of sight for his morning necessities.

As soon as her father was out of sight, Elizabeth caught Canyon's shoulder and pulled him to her for a kiss. It lasted longer than he guessed it would.

"That has to do you all day," he said.

She moaned at him and looked for a comb to do her hair.

They had the coffee for breakfast, then broke camp and were in the saddle again fifteen minutes after rising.

On the horizon they saw a lot of smoke columns and figured it was a town.

"We could use some food and a good meal in the village," Canyon decided. "Any votes against that?"

Hirum and Elizabeth both laughed, and they moved a little faster then, the prospects of a real meal urging them on.

They arrived in the town of Longtree shortly after ten that morning and stopped at a café next to the hotel. Canyon ate a big plate of eggs, fried potatoes, toast, coffee, and a stack of hotcakes. All the while he watched their back trail into the town, but saw no sign of Vickers.

"He couldn't be here yet," Canyon said at last. "Not even if he knew we were coming here and they rode all night."

"Then sit down and enjoy your breakfast and dinner," Hirum said. "You sure we're heading the right direction?"

"Just checked with the man who runs this place. We head a little west and mostly north to Butler, then it's straight north into Kansas City. Can't miss it. More towns up that way, too, the man said."

"Good. More people around, less chance Vickers is going to have to waylay us along here." Hirum said it with conviction, but it faded as he watched Canyon. "You think we have a chance to get away from him free and clear? He was mighty determined to get me and my Betsy gun over to England."

"It would have made him a rich man," Canyon said. "We beat him once, we can do it again. If he catches us."

They didn't waste time in the town. After breakfast they stopped at the general store and bought eight dollars' worth of trail food, mostly canned things as well as two loaves of fresh bread. Then they were moving again, riding out little more than a half-hour after they arrived, now well-fed and ready for a long trip. They angled across some open land, found the road that shot north like a stretched hangman's rope, and vanished into the haze of the morning sunshine.

Hirum rode alongside Canyon now and waved. "Hey there, government man. You say the president actually said he wants to keep my gun in this country?"

"He sure did, Mr. Merchant. My boss in Washington said that President Buchanan was highly concerned that we help you finish your development and then test the gun."

"Ain't that something, Elizabeth? The actual real life president of the whole country. I never been within a hundred miles of a real president. He actually is interested in something I been dreaming about and working on for nigh on to ten years now."

"The army is eager to see it as well, Mr. Merchant. That's partly why we're going to Fort Leavenworth."

Hirum Merchant blinked and looked away. He wiped at his eyes. "I ain't never had much, Canyon O'Grady. Not much book learning. My old pa was a dirt farmer and admitted he wasn't much good at it. I got to know weapons from him. Now, there was a man who could use a breechloader to do just what he wanted.

"I got taken with gunsmithing early. Worked with a man in the closest town. Worked with Old Man Hodkins for five years. Then he booted me out. Said I knew everything he did and I should be making a living at it. I was maybe fourteen, fifteen at the time.

"Nope, Canyon, I never asked for much. But damned if I'm gonna have some wild-assed Englishman steal my gun." He looked up at Canyon. "There now. Had my say. Reckon I run on at the mouth enough to last the rest of the trip."

Elizabeth rode close to her father and put her hand on his shoulder.

They made good time that morning. It was nearly two that afternoon when Canyon sensed trouble. They were riding up the road. It was a wagon track here, wide and with actual ditches dug by the farmers and ranchers alongside to run the rainwater off it. Somebody had floated it with a big heavy drag recently and it would be halfway smooth for a wagon or buggy. The road held a lot of wagon and horseshoe tracks, and now and then some oxen tracks.

The trail here ran straight and true north, and a quarter of a mile ahead it passed right through a cluster of trees. Sycamores, oaks, hickory, and some ash. Canyon saw some dogwood blooming on the near edge.

The road looked like a tunnel going into the woods. From that point they couldn't see through to the other side, although Canyon figured it couldn't be more than a hundred yards at the most. He had an uneasy feeling as they approached it.

Two hundred yards from the woods he saw what he figured might be a metal flash just at the near edge of the woods where the sun came down full.

"Trouble," he shouted. "Swing around the woods. Now!" He jolted his horse through the shallow ditch and into the open countryside to his left, and the other two followed. They had gone no more than ten strides when a rifle boomed from the front of the woods.

"Due west," Canyon shouted as the four horses galloped for all they were worth away from the trap that someone had laid.

Two more rifle shots came then, and Canyon figured they were from muzzle loaders. He was glad they didn't have repeating Spencer rifles. Still, the muzzle loaders could reach out a long way, he knew.

"Bend over your mount," he called. "Make a smaller target that way."

The rifle boomed again, then a new one sounded too quickly to be the same weapon. There were two long guns reaching for them. Canyon heard a shout and looked around. Hirum had nearly fallen off his horse. He hung on to the animal's mane with one hand and with the other had a tight grip on his left shoulder. Blood seeped between his fingers.

"Bastards hit me," Hirum called.

"Keep going," Canyon shouted. "Farther we get away, worse their aim will be."

They rode hard again. Hirum held his saddle, and the three of them spread out a little to make hitting anyone more difficult. The rifles kept shooting behind them, but now the range had grown to six hundred yards and the bullets were not coming as close. At last they rode down into a small depression and were out of sight of the gunmen.

Elizabeth jumped off her mount and helped her father to the ground. Canyon hurried up and checked the wound. It was bad. Hirum was losing a lot of blood. Canyon took his blanket, cut it, ripped it into long strips, and bound the shoulder, pinning Hirum's left arm tightly to his body. The blood soaked into the blanket, but soon dwindled and then stopped.

Elizabeth ripped up a blouse she had brought along and they slipped the blanket strips off and she put a compress of white cloth over the wound, then they bound it with white strips and at last with more of the heavy blanket.

Canyon rushed up to the edge of the little swale and looked at the clump of trees. He could see horses then, five of them; they had grouped and were now riding slowly toward the swale. He checked it. There was no continuing low place, no valley or gully they could ride through and get away safely.

"We'll have to take care of it right here," Canyon said. He looked at the packhorse. "How quickly can I set up your machine gun," Canyon asked.

"Five minutes," Hirum said. Then a gleam came into his eyes. "Yes, by damn! I can help."

They pulled the weapon off the packhorse, set it up a little back from the lip of the gully, then Hirum showed Canyon how to load in the canvas belt of ammunition.

The belt still had over a hundred rounds on it. Canyon ran to the top of the swale and looked over. They were coming forward, still in a close group. He set his mouth. This might be the first actual offensive-defensive use of a machine gun in history.

He had Hirum show him how it worked again. Hirum charged one round into the gun's chamber with his good right hand. "Now all you have to do is pull the trigger and aim through the sights."

Canyon moved the gun forward now, until he could sight just over the top of the depression. He could see the riders. They came forward slowly, all showing rifles. They were still three hundred yards away. He lowered the machine gun onto the tripod and snapped it into place, then squatted behind it and aimed at the oncoming men.

"Do it, Canyon," Hirum called. "It's the only chance we got against five rifles."

Canyon aimed at the center of the men and squeezed the trigger. Before he could get his finger off the metal, six rounds burst forth. He looked up and saw the five men take the slugs. Two horses went down. One man was blown out of his saddle.

Canyon fired again, a ten-round burst. He moved the barrel, sighting on three men who had lunged to the side. He fired six rounds, then six more. Two more of the men went down and one horse broke free, threw his rider, and thundered away.

Canyon could smell the barrel getting hot. He waited for fifteen seconds, then saw one man riding forward straight at him.

Could it be Vickers? Had one of his henchmen rescued the wounded man and brought him here? Canyon aimed and pulled the trigger. His rounds went high. He lowered the sights and fired another six rounds. Two of them struck the horse, but it kept coming forward.

Canyon aimed again and fired a ten-round burst.

He looked up in time to see the rounds blast into the horse's head and the man behind it. The rider took three rounds in the chest and two in his face. He plunged off the dying horse, cartwheeled to the ground, and sprawled in the Missouri dust, dead.

Canyon looked at the last of the five men still alive riding back toward the brush. He lifted the sights and sent two bursts of six rounds at the man, but he vanished into the woods unscathed.

Hirum came up to the weapon and dropped to his knees. He had seen the effective work his invention had accomplished.

Canyon could only kneel there and shake his head.

"Mr. Merchant, this weapon is awesome. It's hellfire! It's a gun any army in the world would spend millions to get. I don't know how I can explain what I feel. We were all dead. I can use that Spencer, but five-to-one is not good odds. Without that machine gun of yours, we'd be ready for a grave about now."

Hirum heard him and nodded. He reached out and touched the handles, let his hand run along the oblong black receiver, and then stared at the mass of spent brass casings on the ground beside the gun.

"I've tested it." He stopped and shook his head. "I've never seen it in a test like that one. Four men, four horses routed and down in less than twenty seconds." Tears ran down his cheeks.

Canyon didn't say a word. It was a time for Hirum Merchant alone. The culmination of ten years of dreaming and working and sacrificing. Ten years of struggle—and his invention worked!

"I had no idea how deadly it could be. Even at three, four hundred yards! It could have reached out a thousand yards just as easy. My God, what a destructive machine!" He brushed at the tears.

Canyon left him there, walked to his horse, and mounted. He wanted to check the bodies. The first he came to was Vickers. He was dead. A few minutes later he found that the other three men were also departed. He rode back and went to the machine gun.

He started to take it apart, but Hirum held up his hand. "There's no rush now, and that barrel would burn your hand. Let's give it a time to cool off."

It was almost an hour later before they could dismantle the gun from the tripod and load it on the packhorse. They left the brass where it was and rode well around the bodies and back to the road north. That night they camped almost twenty miles from the scene of the battle.

Elizabeth had said little as they rode. She had been stunned by the sudden death, shocked by the ease with which the gun killed. Canyon had seen the way she looked at him, then in almost the same way at her father. She would have a lot to say later, he knew.

That night they came into a town near Butler and stayed at the small hotel. They took three rooms, and Canyon paid for them from a money belt he kept around his waist.

They all had supper in the dining room and then went to bed. They would get an early start in the morning.

About midnight, Canyon heard a knock on his door. He drew his revolver and went to the panel. He was still in his pants and socks. "Who is it?" he asked.

"Elizabeth. I have to talk."

He unbolted the door and let her in. She was still in her divided-skirt riding clothes, her eyes red from tears.

"That awful gun," she blurted. "It's a terrible thing. My own father invented it and it killed four men today in about as long as it takes me to tell you this. It's a monster!"

He took her in his arms and let her cry against his shoulder. He knew he'd have to talk to her, but not just yet. He let her cry for five minute, then kissed away the tears and led her to the bed, where they sat down. He brushed at the last of the tears.

"If it wasn't for that machine gun your father invented, you and I would both be dead by now, and your father would be wounded and heading for England with Vickers. That gun your father made saved your life today."

"That gun is made for one reason, only one reason: to kill other human beings. At least a rifle can be used to hunt animals to keep people from starving. A machine gun is made only to be used in war. I hate it."

He kissed her lips, but she didn't respond. "Elizabeth, look at me," he commanded. She turned, her eyes red, nose with a drip. "Your father invented the machine gun. Someone, somewhere was bound to do it sooner or later. I've heard it talked about for years. Someone would do it. There is no way to stop progress. The Indians say the train will kill off the buffalo, and it probably will.

"White settlers kept pushing the Indians back from the East Coast to the Mississippi, and now they are being forced farther and farther west. That's progress and it can't be stopped. Neither can the invention of the machine gun be stopped.

"Your father did it. He deserves the credit and the financial rewards. The U.S. Army deserves to be the first in the world to be armed with it. Tomorrow or the next day we'll get to Fort Leavenworth. Then you can go your way and forget all about what you saw today, and about the machine gun. I won't let you spoil this moment of triumph for your father."

Elizabeth slapped him. Her face was hard and angry. "You don't understand. That damn gun killed four men today so quickly I could hardly count the bodies falling. That is monstrous, unspeakable!"

He caught her arms and held her tightly. She began to cry again. The sobs came and she wailed and cried and after ten minutes got it all out.

Canyon kissed her and she tried to respond but couldn't.

"What are you going to do tomorrow?" he asked.

"I . . . I don't know. I guess I'll go along with you to the fort. There I'll make up my mind what to do." She sighed and a little tremor ran through her from the crying. She caught her breath and sighed again.

Canyon kissed her lips gently, then with more force, and at last she kissed him back. He touched one of her breasts and she pulled away.

"No, not tonight. I have too much to think about. Let me work it out the rest of the night and tomorrow."

He nodded, kissed her cheek, and led her to the door. They went outside and to her room, where she pushed the door open and went in. The lamp was still burning.

"Good night," he said. "Try not to think about it too much." She nodded and closed the door.

Back in his own room, Canyon thought about it as well. Yes, she was right. A machine gun had only one purpose: to kill human beings. There was no other reasonable use for it. It was a war machine. But since men always had wars, new machines had to be invented.

For the moment the logic of that idea confused him. He rolled over and went to sleep and didn't wake up until nearly daylight the next morning.

10

Canyon got up, shaved, put on a clean shirt, checked the loads in his six-gun, then finished dressing and went to see if Elizabeth was awake.

She let him in at his knock. She wore only her chemise and skirt. He tried not to let the sight of her breasts pushing out against the soft cloth excite him.

Elizabeth put on her blouse and buttoned it to the neck, then she tried to smile, but it just wasn't working. "I'm still confused and hurt and angry. I haven't said a thing to Pa. I figure that I shouldn't. Is that right?"

She looked up at him, her pale-green eyes seemed as wide as dinner plates, her chin quivered; she moved, and her blond hair trembled around her face and shoulders.

"Yes, Elizabeth, I don't think you should worry your father with your feelings right now. First we have to get him and his invention to Fort Leavenworth. Then will be time enough to think it through."

She gave a peck on the cheek and they headed for breakfast. Hirum wasn't in his room and they found him waking up over a cup of coffee in the small dining room. He seemed lost in his own thoughts as they ate, and the three talked little. They left the hotel well before seven o'clock and headed due north up the country road.

Elizabeth rode slightly behind the two men, who talked of guns and ammunition and what could and couldn't be done with a Spencer rifle.

"Give me a good breechloader and let me measure my own powder and lead, and I'll beat your Spencer any day for accuracy and power and range," Hirum said. "I can load for accurate shooting up to fifteen hundred yards, damn near a mile."

"But for your one shot I can get off at least eight," Canyon said. "If I rushed it, I could probably fire fifteen before you got your second round fired."

"Lead all over the place don't make no difference if you don't hit what you aim at," Hirum argued.

They kept at it for the next hour, talking over the benefits of one weapon over another and how slow the army was in getting their service revolvers converted to solid cartridges instead of percussion.

They topped a small rise in the road and ahead they saw a coach coming toward them; it had red and green sides.

"First stagecoach we've seen around here," Canyon said as the rig came closer. It had two men on the high front seat and was pulled by an unmatched team of four. On this level ground four could haul the rig with no trouble.

Canyon had ridden a lot of stages lately, and trains in the east. He preferred the trains. The coach came forward and now he could see that it was not one of the big Concords. It looked more like one of the Owensboro mountain stages, but he couldn't be sure.

The three of them went to single-file along the road to give the rig room to pass. Instead of keeping going, it came to a stop beside them and the driver called.

"Hey, looks like I'm plumb lost. You gents know where I might find the thriving little city of Butler, Missouri?"

"Sure, it's to the south a ways," Canyon said. Then he saw the two pistols aiming through the curtains over the windows and he whipped his hand down for his six-gun.

He never made it. A shot from one of the pistols

slammed into his chest high up, blasting him off his horse and dumping him hard into the dirt. He was stunned and didn't move. That probably saved his life.

"Hands up, you other two," a voice with a German accent said. "Now is no time to try to be brave. Old man, hands on your head. Fräulein, keep your hands where we can see them. We do not wish to hurt either of you."

Three men got out of the coach and pulled the two Merchants off their horses. They hustled them into the seats after stripping the six-gun away from Hirum.

Their horses were tied on the back, including the pack-horse. One of the men looked at Canyon, evidently decided he was dead, and whacked his big bay horse, which went prancing into the field at the side of the road.

The men got back in the coach and the driver turned it around by going into the shallow ditch and back on the road, then moved back north the direction from which they had come.

Several minutes passed and Canyon came fully conscious. He had been drifting in and out of lucidity for five minutes. He remembered being shot, falling, then seeing bits and pieces of the drama as the Merchants were put into the coach. A fly buzzed around his chest and looked down and saw the trace of blood there.

He should be dead. Small caliber of some kind. He could see north along the road and could just make out a dust trail as the coach and trailing horses went out of sight.

First, was he alive? Canyon knew he felt half-dead. The round must have missed most vital parts inside his chest. His heart was pumping, he could breathe, but the round might still have hit a lung. He pushed himself to a sitting position.

The world spun and took on a serious shade of black, then cleared up and he could see plainly again. He was hurt bad, he knew that. His horse? He looked around and saw her munching on some grass twenty yards away.

He called to her. The sound of his voice was strange, and when he called, it was as if someone had struck him in the chest with a hammer. The horse paid no attention to him. He checked his holster. His big Colt was still there.

Could he stand? Could he walk? He went to his hands and knees and tried to stand. He got to one foot, but when he tried to push up, he blacked out and tumbled to the ground. It took him three tries before he could stand.

The land tipped and slid and wavered for another minute before it settled down. He took one halting step toward the horse, then one more. The shallow ditch beside the road proved to be a major obstacle.

Canyon fell down the first step he took into the ditch. He crawled to the other side, stood, and then tried to figure out how to get around a small shrub that grew in front of him. At last he took a shuffling step to one side and mastered the problem.

It took Canyon a full five minutes to walk the twenty yards to his horse, who saw him coming and rolled one big brown eye, then walked six feet away to better grass.

He touched her hind quarters first and patted the big animal so she would not bolt away. She didn't. At last he caught the saddle with both hands and only then did he realize that he would have to lift himself into the saddle.

How in hell could he do that? Just reaching for the saddle had sent a dozen sharp knives stabbing through the nerve endings in his upper chest. Had the bullet come out his back? He had no way of knowing.

Up, dammit! Up! Sweat beaded his forehead. He had lost his hat somewhere. Canyon took a deep breath, felt new pains in his lungs, and slowly lifted his left foot toward the stirrup. Without the stirrup he was utterly lost. He had no idea how far it was to the next town or settlement, but he would never to be able to walk there.

Higher, dammit, higher! His foot wavered six inches below the iron. He pushed it higher and bellowed in pain. Higher! Another inch. Another inch.

At last his toe nudged the stirrup and he pushed it forward. He had his foot solidly planted in the stirrup. His chest felt like one large ulcerous, open wound. He even looked down at the bullet hole and the spot of blood. Surprising how little the entry hole of a bullet bleeds.

He felt sweat run down his forehead, past his nose, and touch his upper lip.

For the moment he stood there, one leg in the stirrup. He didn't want to think about the pain it would cause to try to lift up and throw his right leg over the saddle. Horrendous.

Then he remembered the gun, that damn machine gun, that fantastic weapon that could make the United States the world's leading military power. Or that could be used to crush our forces by massive numbers of British or German machine-gun brigades.

Canyon bellowed a roar of rage and pain and at the same time surged upward, the sense of the roar giving him added strength to hoist himself upward and then to push his leg over.

His chest screamed in agony. His head exploded in unvoiced billows of pain. Somewhere in his chest or back, the lead slug gave him another debilitating roaring wave of torture.

Then his leg was over the saddle and he settled into the familiar leather seat.

"Oh, damn!" He gasped for breath, tried to quiet the blasting, surging pain in his chest. It wouldn't go away. The reins had dropped to the ground as the horse grazed. He reached and with another spasm of agony caught the reins and brought them over the bay's head.

She turned and watched him with one large brown

eye. He patted her neck and she turned, ready. More ready than he was. He turned her head back to the roadway and felt each step she took. The small jolts of her walking had become quickly lost in the sense of riding before. Now each pounding of hoof to ground jolted him and sent new icy shards of pain streaking into his nervous system.

By the time they got the twenty-five yards to the wagon road, tears streamed down his face. He couldn't stop them. Never had one bullet wound caused him so much pain. Why? He had no idea. He turned the bay north and began to walk her slowly in that direction along the road.

With slothlike speed he realized that the stage coach had not been a stage at all, but simply a private coach hired for the purpose to surprise them and to kill him and capture the gun and its creator.

They captured Elizabeth, too. Damn!

Canyon frowned trying to remember the bits and pieces of conversation he heard as he wandered in and out of consciousness as he lay half-dead in the dirt.

"Yes, they spoke with a German accent." he said out loud. He looked around, but there was no one to hear him. But he had killed the three Germans who attacked them before.

"Doppelgänger," he said out loud. He was getting used to hearing his own voice. The Germans would have two teams tracking the gun. Using typical German efficiency, they would put the second team to work when the first was eliminated. Damn the Germans! His eyes filmed over again and the dull gray cloud hovered over the horizon, but with a conscious effort he pushed it back, jolted it away, and kept his seat in the saddle. He would not pass out again. He would not!

Canyon kicked the bay and she moved out faster now, walking down the road with a new purpose. Germans . . . Germans. How would they operate? What would they do? They had the gun and the inventor. They would make him demonstrate it, or fire it themselves.

The Germans probably sent at least one gunsmith on the group to steal the weapon. He would know if they got the real machine gun and if it would work. So first they would test it. What next?

The Germans were methodical people. He guessed that the gunsmith would find a hotel somewhere and make detailed drawings of the gun so there would be no danger of losing the design. His looking at it would nail it down in his thoughts, but he would want every detail of the design down on paper too. That would take time, two or three days.

Yes, the Germans would go to the next town with a hotel, settle in, and make their drawings of the gun. They probably would have already test-fired it before then.

Canyon's next move was to find the bastards who shot him, kill them all, and take back the gun and the captives.

Simple. If he could stay in the saddle that long without falling unconscious or dying.

Twice the first mile he nearly fell. Twice he grabbed on to the bay's mane and kept in the saddle. He was leaning over the mane by the time he negotiated the next three miles. Then, ahead another mile or two he saw smoke lifting into the quiet air. A small town.

He walked his mount into the crossroads town and stopped in front of two old men sitting outside the hardware store. "Gents, wondering if you saw a rig with red and green sides come into town an hour or so ago?"

"I might have, might not," one of the old men said. He had a full beard, stained brown on one corner from tobacco juice. He squinted up at Canyon and grinned, showing gums and no teeth.

The other man laughed, a high cackle that irritated Canyon, but he was in no position to be choosy about his informants. The second man was clean-shaven, his face sunken like his chest, his hands drawn dry skin over bones that could be counted.

He nodded at last. " 'Pears I did see that bunch. Most of them were jabbering away in German. I know some German. They wanted to stop, but the main man on the driver's seat asked only how to get to the closest railroad station."

"We told him Kansas City, due north. He was a real gent. He tossed us a quarter. Now, if'n we had another quarter, we could go over to Annie's and get ourselves some beers."

Canyon dug into his pocket, gasped as it made him move his upper arm and his chest, but found a quarter. He flipped it in the air and caught it.

"One more question. Is there a sawbones in town? I picked up a mite bit of lead."

The younger of the two with the beard stood and scowled. "Hell, son, that's me. Thought you looked a little peaked. My place is just across the street. Not a lot of call for medicine these days."

A half-hour later Canyon came back to his horse. The doctor had not found the slug. Said in two or three days it would be easier to find due to some swelling some-where. He patched up Canyon's chest, put on some salve, and gave him two shots of whiskey, then helped him out to his horse.

"Like I say, you need some rest and a surgeon to dig out that slug."

Canyon looked at him sternly.

"But like I say, I'll take your two-dollar fee and keep my trap shut." He chuckled. "Damnation, wish I was that tough again. Just dreaming, I reckon."

A while later, Canyon rode out of town feeling better. He had a pint of whiskey in his saddlebag, some solid food in his stomach, and a long ride ahead. The next town was more than eight miles due north. Couldn't miss it.

He rode. Eight miles would have taken him an hour

on a good horse—if he was feeling good. Now it took him two hours, and he was glad to see it. He had not fallen off or even blacked out, but he came close once.

Canyon came in town slowly, checked with three people before he talked to someone who had seen the big coach with the red and green sides. They said it had stopped at the hotel. The rig wasn't parked in front or in back of the two-story hostelry. Canyon got down off his horse where he could use the boardwalk as a one-foot-high step, and tied her up.

The clerk in the hotel had been positive.

"Yes, sir, they were here. A man with a German accent. He said he wanted six rooms and I told him I had only three left. We talked awhile and finally I rented him a small house we own and rent by the day or week. It's about two blocks down behind the livery stable. Nice little place, white with a green trim. Only one like it in town. You need a room?"

"Maybe later, not right now. How long they been in the house?"

"Since two o'clock. That's about two hours now, I'd say."

Canyon forgot and turned quickly, grunted as the pain stabbed through his chest. He nodded at the clerk and headed out the door at an easy walk, trying not to jolt on his heels the way he sometimes did.

On the way to his horse O'Grady checked his six-gun. He had five rounds ready to go, and the Spencer. Fast firing might come in handy this time. They had wanted six rooms. That meant at least four or five men against him. So be it. He had never intended to live forever anyway.

Canyon rode slowly down toward the livery, then eased up and looked both ways. He could see the white house with the green trim south of the livery stables. One house across the street. Other than that, no cover. Be damn hard to sneak up on the place. He'd have to wait until after dark.

He looked again but couldn't spot the big coach. Maybe it was behind the house. He rode a block away from the livery, then a block south so he could get another angle on the white house. Now he could see the backyard. There was a shack there and an outhouse and a small barn big enough for about three horses. But no coach. Maybe they left it somewhere else.

Three horses were picketed outside the barn. The German guests were at home.

Canyon rode back to a solitary elm tree growing beside the street and sat down in the shade. He was having less trouble now getting up and down from his mount. He wished he could sneak up to the house and know for sure that's who was inside and find out what they were doing to Elizabeth and Hirum. They probably wouldn't hurt Elizabeth as long as they needed Hirum's cooperation.

He didn't want to think what would happen once the German gunsmiths had their drawings and understood the mechanics of the machine gun. Then Hirum would be of no use to them. They would take the train for the East Coast and grab a sailing ship for Germany. At least that's probably what they planned to do. He would cause them some problems.

Canyon stared at the white house, now over three hundred yards away. Even if they looked out the window, they couldn't identify him. He was just another man with a horse. He made sure that four of his extra tubes for the Spencer carbine were filled with their regulation seven rounds.

Then he leaned back against the elm and closed his eyes. He heard a rig roll by and saw that it was a light buggy with a man and a woman in it. A gray pulled it. No trouble.

Canyon catnapped for two hours. Whenever he opened his eyes, he checked the white house. There was no activity. Only a light blue plume of smoke from

121

the kitchen chimney. Somebody, probably Elizabeth, must be getting the men some supper.

Fine idea.

He stood slowly and grabbed his bay's reins and walked two blocks to a small café. He took the Spencer with him inside, slung muzzle down. It was too fine a weapon to leave in the saddle boot for some light-fingered galoot.

Canyon ordered a steak and all the fixings. He wanted it rare and it came in a few minutes, seared on the outside and blood-red inside. He couldn't have done better himself.

As he rested and as he ate, he let his inner mind work on the problem of the green-trimmed white house. He couldn't storm the place. If they never went outside, he couldn't pick them off one by one. What else? If he had some black powder and some fuse, he could set a good-sized bomb off in the backyard and gain an advantage.

The idea came to him as he worked through possibilities. He grinned, paid his check, and went back out to his horse at the rail. It was dusk and would be dark in another hour. No reason to wait much after dark this time.

The task of rescuing Hirum and Elizabeth would take some time. He would also have to find the drawings and take them with him or burn them in the stove. Taking them would be the safest way. Then the gun would need to be packed on board the horse, and he would need the animals for his two rescued persons. Yes, it was going to take more time to get everything from that house than he wanted it to.

His solution would have to be permanent. If there was another way, he would find it. The more he thought on the problem, the faster ideas came. First he would get the horses out of the small barn and have them saddled and ready to go before his attack as such began. Yes. He would free the horses first, then the riders.

He could walk upright now with only a slight pain.

He knew there would be a reckoning. That slug had to be dug out by someone within three days, or he'd be in bad trouble. Lead and human flesh had a way of killing each other.

As it grew fully dark, Canyon rode down toward the white house, then past it, and checked the barn. Yes, three or four or five horses in there. He went back thirty yards from the front door and tied his mount to a scrub hazelnut bush.

Canyon picked up the Spencer from the saddle boot and made sure his big Colt was in leather. Then he circled around the house and barn and came up in back of it.

He was just about at the side door of the barn when the house screen door slammed. A dark blob came from the house and walked quickly to the outhouse. Canyon waited. A few moments later the outhouse door swung open and a man went back into the small house.

Canyon slipped inside the barn, found the roan that Elizabeth rode, and threw on the saddle and cinched it in place. He tied the roan beside the back door, then found another horse and saddle and brought them up as well.

Canyon had no idea which horse had been used as a pack animal. He found the heavy leather carrier and lifted it on the back of a horse. It didn't bolt for the door or kick the wall, so Canyon cinched the pack-saddle device in place.

He was sure the gun itself was inside being inspected, taken apart, studied.

Canyon watched the house for a minute, then led the three horses out the back door of the barn, swung them in a fifty-yard arc around the house, and tied them near his own horse.

Canyon returned to the back of the house and the shed. He looked inside the eight-foot-square building. It had been used for grain and wood and hay. Good.

He looked at the moon. It was out bright. Nothing

he could do about that. He pulled the wad of sulfur matches from his pocket and propped the door open. He broke off two of the sulfur matches and grinned.

"Gonna be a hot time in the old town tonight," he whispered, and struck the matches.

11

The two matches Canyon O'Grady lighted flared into flames and he lay them carefully at two places in the straw in the shed. He waited to be sure the flames caught and held, then he slipped out the side door away from the house and ran quickly to the front of the house.

He watched the fire get a good hold on the shack and then burst out one of the windows. He threw a large rock against the side of the house and saw men slip out the front door to investigate the noise. Soon he heard someone in back.

"Fire," someone yelled at the back of the house.

Canyon watched until he saw five men rush out the back door, then he went to the front door and slipped in through the unlocked panel.

He had his gun out but didn't need it. Hirum sat tied to a chair in the front room. Canyon's knife cut the bindings quickly.

"Drawings," Canyon said, pointing to the papers littering the dining-room table beside the coal-oil lamp. "Get them all, everyone. Where's Elizabeth?"

"First bedroom, over there," Hirum said.

Canyon jumped to the door, saw that it was locked from the outside. He jerked the bolt open and pushed the door inward.

Elizabeth looked up in alarm. Then she saw him and smiled and raced to the door.

"Outside, both of you. There are horses about twenty

yards down the street to the left. Get there and ride north. I'll find you. Where is the gun?''

Hirum pointed to where it sat on its tripod next to the table.

Canyon grinned. "Then let's all leave, right now. Let them be surprised when the come back inside.''

Hirum lifted the gun off the tripod and put it on his shoulder. He had grabbed the German's drawings and stuffed them inside his shirt. Canyon caught the tripod, folded it, and carried it in one hand toward the front door. Hirum and Elizabeth were outside the front door when Canyon heard someone storm in the back door.

Canyon waited by the front door. He saw a man race into the room with a six-gun in his hand. Canyon put two rounds into the man's chest and he slammed backward.

Then Canyon ran for the horses. Elizabeth and her father were mounted by the time he got there. He pushed up into his saddle with the tripod. He saw a form race forward from the house, he lifted the Spencer from the boot and slammed a shot into the spot where the man stood. The man yelped in alarm and the next round blew him away from the side of the house and onto the ground.

"Move," Canyon called, and they rode down the town's dirt street. It headed directly west. "Doesn't matter where we go just so it's away from here," he called.

When they were a mile out of town, Canyon could not hear any pursuit. He stopped and they laced the machine gun and the mount onto the packhorse and tied them down securely.

"North now," Canyon said. "I put two of them down. It depends if I got the leader of the group or not. Were they all Germans or had they hired on some local guns?''

"Three were Germans, the other two were Americans," Elizabeth said. "I kept scolding them for helping foreigners."

"Did they have a gunsmith along?" Canyon asked.

"Oh, yes, a very bright young man."

"Did he understand the principle of your mechanism?"

"He was starting to. He hadn't had long to work on the gun. He was making detailed drawings with measurements and parts on all of it."

"Will he remember what he learned?"

"Maybe, maybe not. He didn't get to the vital element, what makes the whole thing function. He has some bits and pieces."

"Good, we might still come out on top of this little international race yet."

They settled down and rode, working on roads that led back to the main north-south highway. It wasn't hard to recognize it when they came to it. Here and there it had been graded up higher than the surrounding fields, which were showing some farming areas now and fences for livestock.

"Starting to look downright civilized around here," Canyon said.

They rode for another hour through the night. Then Canyon's nose started to twitch. "Are we coming toward another town? Mr. Merchant, do you know this area?"

"Seems to me the next town is about six or seven miles from that one we were in. If I remember right. We could be almost there."

They found it over a next low rise of the land, coming down from a hundred feet or so into a gentle valley on the plains. It was on a junction with a good road that led to the east.

"Anyone want to stay at a hotel tonight?" Canyon asked.

"We should, Elizabeth said. "Since both Pa and I left without our bedrolls or my little carpetbag of clothes. What I'm wearing is everything in the world I own."

They rode into the town singly and registered at the hotel as individuals ten minutes apart. That would make it harder for the Germans or anyone else to know they were there. When they were all inside, they came into the hall and then met in Hirum's room. They had carried the machine gun up there and hid it under the bed.

Hirum looked at Canyon and a frown covered his face. "I figured you were dead. I saw that man shoot you right in the chest back there on the road when the coach came. You went down and didn't move. I don't understand."

Canyon sat down on the bed and groaned. "You're right, I should be dead. An inch either way and I would be. As it is, I've got a broken rib and a bullet somewhere in back of my lung. It put me down and unconscious. When I came to, I could see the coach racing off. I just decided I wasn't going to let them get away with stealing your gun."

"That takes more than deciding. You know that bullet has to come out in another day or two."

"I know. We'll do it at Fort Leavenworth. Both of you all right?"

Elizabeth nodded. "They wouldn't touch me as long as Pa was there and they needed him. But I could tell . . ." She took a deep breath. "I'm glad you got there when you did."

Hirum nodded. "I had a little talk with the German guy. Warned him that if anybody even touched Elizabeth, I'd throw my gun in the river. He gave strict orders. He didn't know a barrel from a tripod. The short one was the gunsmith."

"We all can use some sleep. We'll get going a little later in the morning. I want to talk to the law in this town. Hopefully it'll be a county seat and I can get some help from the sheriff with an escort on into Kansas City."

"Sounds good to me," Hirum said. "I'm getting blamed tired of getting kidnapped and shot at and such."

"Time for me to get some sleep," Canyon said. "Put the chair behind your doorknob to keep out wandering Germans." He demonstrated pushing the top of the chair under the handle with the chair sitting only on the back legs. "Anybody coming in has to break the chair, and that makes a lot of racket." Canyon handed his revolver to Hirum. "Keep this handy just in case. I'll keep the Spencer. Elizabeth, you still have that little iron of yours?"

She showed him the pocket she had sewn into the long divided skirt she wore. "They didn't even think to look for it back there. I was trying to figure out when to use it."

Canyon nodded, went to the door. "Good night. See you both in the morning."

He went into his room and lit the lamp. The bed wasn't the best but it would be better than the ground. They were all on the second floor, which helped keep anyone from breaking in the windows.

He took off his boots and checked the Spencer to be sure there was a round in the chamber. He sat down on the bed and pulled at his shirt when he heard a knock on his door. He opened it and Elizabeth stepped inside quickly and closed the door and threw the bolt in place.

"We need to talk," she said. She sat down on the bed and motioned him to sit beside her. "I've been thinking about what you said about the gun, about Pa's invention and how much it means to him. I've also been thinking about the wonderful way we made love."

She reached up and kissed his lips, clinging to them a moment. Then she came away and stared straight ahead. "I still don't like the machine gun. I saw what it did. I could imagine it being used against a hundred men charging across a valley. It's . . . it's just terrible." She turned and stared at him. "But I've about decided that I don't have to think about the bad things that it can do. A rifle can kill people. A kitchen butcher knife can kill people just as easily.

"So that brings us to the other half of my problem." She began to unbutton her blouse. "Pa is in his room and we're in our room and I want to feel you with me again. I know you're hurt, but we'll figure out how to make love without hurting you anymore. Can we do that?"

She kissed him again and washed his lips with her tongue. Canyon laughed softly and put his arms around her. She had her blouse open then and one of his hands crept inside and curved around her bare breast.

"Elizabeth, I think we'll be able to figure out some way so I don't hurt too much."

"Wonderful!" Her light-green eyes sparkled in the lamplight as she kissed him gently. "Now I'd like you to undress me. Do it just any way you want to. I want to feel you taking my clothes off and know that I'm all yours, totally, completely, without reservation of any kind. I think that means I love you."

He kissed her gently and caressed her breasts like they were art objects of great price. Then he kissed her lips and began to take off her clothes.

Her blouse was first, then he pushed his head under the loose chemise and found her breasts and kissed them until Elizabeth was panting and moaning with urgent desire. He chewed on one breast and brought her nipple up to hardness. He could feel her orbs pulsating and growing hotter and hotter.

Canyon slipped the chemise off over her head, feeling a stab of pain in his chest, but ignoring it. His own hot blood would soon dull the pain.

He smiled at Elizabeth's angel face and pushed her gently down on the bed on her back. He lay half on top of her and devoured her breasts again. Gently he spread her legs under him and touched her crotch and she jolted into a hard climax, bouncing him around on the bed, shaking and shivering and letting spasm after spasm rip through her tender body. She moaned in rapture and her face twisted from pain into delight. When the last of the spasms rattled through her delicious young body, she opened her eyes and looked up at him.

"How long have I been missing out on such a marvelous, fantastic experience?"

"It didn't exist until you created it, so enjoy." He kissed her nose and urged her hips off the bed so he could slip down her skirt. She grabbed at it a moment in reflex, but when he kissed her hand she let it go.

Canyon slid her skirt down and off her legs. She had come into the room barefoot. His hands worked up and down her legs for a minute and then she sat up.

"Now I get to undress you. Are you hurting?"

"Not now. When I get good and hard, I don't feel much of anything else." He put her hand on his crotch, where his erection was full and pressing against his pants.

"Good, let's get him out of that trap he's in. Poor baby in there all held down tight."

She opened the fly on his pants and then his belt and pulled down his pants until he sprang upward, ready for action.

"Oh, my, what a dandy," she said, then bent and kissed the head before she went on undressing him. She smiled as she perched on the bed on her knees. She was wearing only her white loose drawers and her breasts swung freely as she moved.

"You do know you're the first man I've ever undressed? A man is so marvelous, so wonderful, all trim chest and flat belly and muscles in his back that ripple and bulge. Did I tell you I've always been partial to redheads? I wondered if they had red chest hair and if the hair on their legs was red."

She laughed and looked at him. "I also wondered if their crotch hair was red, too. Now I know it is." She laughed again, a nervous titter that made her more adorable. She pushed close to him, her breasts crushed against his naked chest, and she kissed him passionately.

"Darling, wonderful Canyon O'Grady. I'm nervous, you know that? Here I sit all bare on top with my breasts uncovered and my skirt off an in a man's bedroom undressing him, and I want so desperately for him to make love to me—but I'm still nervous and feel shy and inexperienced."

He hugged her tightly, kissed her again, and then leaned away from her a little so he could fondle her perky, full breasts.

"Being a little nervous never hurt a thing. You are beautiful with a marvelous sexy body that any man would kill for, and you're here because you want to be, so just enjoy it. We sometimes have to live life as it comes, because the next day things can change and it might never be the same, or as good again."

"Kiss my breasts. I love that feeling."

He did, kissing them, licking them, feeling their heat surge, and at last chewing on her nipples until she surged into another climax, shaking and rattling until he thought she might break apart.

At last the climax rattled away and she looked up and grinned.

"Oh, glory, that is so wonderful!" Then she was all over him, pulling down his pants, pushing his shirt off his shoulders, and then pulling down his short underwear and squealing as his manhood angled up, still and hard and pulsating.

She dropped on the bed on her back. "Lay on top of me," she urged. "I love it when you mash me down into the mattress." Her delicate fingers touched the bandage on his upper chest. "Does it hurt now?"

"Can't feel a thing but this marvelous lady who is almost naked and lying in my bed." He grinned and eased down on top of her. She had spread her legs and he settled between them, feeling her cotton drawers. He reached down and pulled on them and she helped him work them off.

Her eyes sparkled as she watched him. Tears edged into them and she blinked. "Sometimes I cry when I'm so happy I just can't stand it," she told him.

"Like now?"

"Exactly, right now. Like living life to the fullest while we can, because it might change tomorrow. A very handsome young man told me that. I had no idea he could be so beautiful and such a wonderful lover and at the same time so wise."

She pulled his mouth down to hers. The kiss lasted a long time, and as it did, she pushed his hips up and then brought them down so his hardness pressed tightly against her crotch.

"Wonderful lover, right now," she whispered. "Right now, there couldn't be a better time. I want him deep, deep inside me!"

He pushed a hand down between them. She was wet and ready. He massaged her outer labia a moment to spread her juices, then edged into her slot and worked in slowly until he was firmly connected to her.

"Oh, Lord! Oh, Lord," Elizabeth cried.

They didn't talk then. He began to move and she countered his motion, opposing it, building the tension. Before he knew it, Elizabeth raced into another climax, nearly bouncing him out of her and pushing them close to the edge of the narrow bed.

She finished the spasms and looked at him wide-eyed, then ripped into another one and he went with her this time, jolting his juices deep into her, and that triggered her again. When they both climaxed together at last, they fell on the bed in a confusion of arms and legs, panting for air.

"Oh, glory," Elizabeth said. She closed her eyes and rested but clung to him, binding them together.

When at last they came back to reality, she looked up and smiled. "Is this what it would be like being married? I mean, we could make love just anytime we wanted to for as long as we wanted to. Every night, at noon times, maybe when we woke up in the morning.''

Canyon laughed. ''At that rate I'd be worn out in about two days and not able to perform for a week. Remember the man is the producer in this case. We can't go on forever.''

''Oh, yes. Oh, I understand. Well, I guess once a day would be enough for a while. In the evening with everything all cozy and warm and tucked in somewhere.''

''Whatever happened to that wild time outdoors on a nice grassy bank of a chattering stream?''

''That, too.'' She frowned. ''Why do I get hungry after we make love?''

''You're just a growing girl.''

She nodded. ''At least I'm getting a little new view of my pa's work. I don't know what I thought he was working on. He must have told me about it. I guess I thought a gun was a gun.''

''So what are you going to do?''

''I don't know. I haven't thought it through far enough yet. I need more time. I'm not going to tell him what I really think right now, that's for sure. When we get to the army fort and he's safe, then there will be time to sort things out.''

''Your father is going to be rich and famous. He deserves it. He's done something that thousands of gunmakers around the world have been trying to do for ten or fifteen years.''

''I just didn't realize how important it was. I kind of got the idea that Pa didn't really appreciate how big an advancement this is. He's just done what he wanted to do without thinking what it would mean or what the gun could do.''

''I agree. But he's starting to see now that everyone is trying to steal him and his invention. Our job is to get him and the gun safely to Fort Leavenworth.''

She grinned. "Hey, enough of the serious talk. Are you ready to make love again?"

Canyon O'Grady laughed. "No, not yet." He pulled away from her and sat up on the bed. "I need to look at your marvelous slender body, your wonderful breasts, and that beautiful face. Sometimes I can't believe that you're sitting here beside me."

"I'm really here, Canyon, and if you're not careful, you may have a hard time getting rid of me. I know," she said, holding up her hands. "You told me you're a traveling man, that you move around the whole country working for the government. I know. Maybe I could come with you, or even just wait for you to come home now and then."

He shushed her with a kiss and they rolled over on the bed and giggled. "You are too, ready again."

Three more times that night they made love, and it wasn't until nearly four in the morning before Elizabeth slipped into her dress. He stopped her and looked at the wounds on her thigh. The holes were sealed over and healing well.

"They don't hurt almost at all anymore," she said. "Just when I try to run too fast." She finished putting on the dress, then hurried down the hall to her own room.

Canyon lay on his bed for a moment, still seduced with the soft, sweet scent of her and the smell of her hair. That was quite a lady. When the time came, it was going to be hard to tell her that indeed he was a traveling man and he had to stay unencumbered. It would be hard, but he would figure out a way. That was part of his job as a United States agent.

That decided, Canyon O'Grady turned over and went to sleep at once.

12

Before breakfast the next morning, Canyon had a talk with the deputy on duty at the local jail.

"Sorry, this ain't the county seat, that'd be Harrisonville. I'm just a local deputy marshal and I can't help you nohow. We're still about thirty-five to forty miles or so from Kansas City. I don't reckon you can get any help between here and there. Sheriff in the next county is short on deputies right now as well."

"Yeah, well, it was a try," Canyon said. "Maybe I'll get lucky." On the way back to the hotel he thought of hiring a few gunhands from the local saloon. But he would have no idea what kind of men he was contracting. He shook his head and decided to work the back roads and go as fast as they could.

They had a quick breakfast, then met in Hirum's room.

"Before we go another step, tell me about this weapon," Canyon said. "I've seen it fire and I've lugged it around, but I don't know anything about it."

Hirum lifted the machine gun to the bed and began explaining.

"It's a single-barrel gun, not like the Gatling with six to twelve barrels. That makes it much simpler from a mechanical standpoint; fewer things can go wrong.

"It's forty-six inches long and weighs twenty-eight pounds, three or four times what a good rifle weighs. The barrel is twenty-six inches long. You know about the water cooling jacket I'm going to put on it to keep the barrel from overheating.

"It fires six hundred rounds a minute with an effective range of fifteen hundred yards. She stands on a tripod and uses a canvas belt to feed the rounds in.

"That's about it. The whole thing functions automatically because of the recoil principle of the receiver."

Canyon nodded. "I even understood some of that. All right, now we wrap the weapon in our saddle blankets and carry it down so we're sure nobody sees it. Then we get out of town as soon as we can."

They left the hotel one by one. The men met behind the hotel, where they loaded the weapon on the packhorse. They had left the animals in a small stable behind the hotel that night and moved out as soon as they could, again going singly and meeting just outside of the small town. Then they headed north.

All morning Canyon had been trying to decide which would be the better plan: to stick to the most heavily traveled road, or to cut out through the country and avoid the roads.

He hadn't decided when they came to the road north. A sign told them that Harrisonville was four miles to the northwest. They moved along the road at a brisk pace. Now Canyon kept a sharp lookout ahead and behind them.

He had not forgotten about Smith and Barnes. They hadn't put in a second appearance. Perhaps the pair and their hired guns had lost the trail. Canyon knew it would not be a hard track to follow if someone really tried and had a little bit of cash to spread around.

No, Smith and Barnes would be along somewhere in the next forty miles or so. They might even make a try for the gun after the trio got to Kansas City. However, there Canyon could call on help from his long-time friend who was now the chief constable of that city.

He rode and watched ahead and behind.

Two hours out, he figured they had made about ten miles. A long way to go. They had passed through Harrisonville on side streets, not hitting the main stem.

"That will make it harder for anyone to follow us," Canyon explained.

By eleven they came to a small stream and some brushy woods filled with a lot of ash and hickory.

Elizabeth whispered to her father and rode into the brush until she was out of sight.

"Nature calls," Hirum said. He shook his head. "I sure do have one pretty daughter, don't you think so, Canyon?"

"Yes, indeed, Mr. Merchant. Pretty as a butterfly."

Hirum smiled. "I was hoping that you'd noticed. Time she was getting married and settled down. Not that I'm thinking about grabbing a shotgun or anything, but you two have been traveling alone for a few days . . . and nights."

Before Canyon could respond, he heard a gunshot, then another, and Elizabeth screamed. He dug heels into horseflesh and jolted toward the woods, pulling the six-gun from leather as he charged through the thin brush to the heaver section.

He came into the thicker woods and found Elizabeth's handkerchief on the ground. At the same time a rifle cracked and a bullet slammed close to him. Canyon whirled his horse and pounded through the brush ten feet the other way, then stopped.

"Smart, damn smart of you," a voice boomed from somewhere in the brush.

Canyon couldn't even tell from what direction the sound came. "Who are you?" he called.

'Don't matter. What does matter is that we got the little lady. Her name is Elizabeth Merchant, and right now we got something you want. We aren't about to get into a shooting match with you again. All we want is the gun the good Mr. Hirum Merchant has.

"He's free to go unharmed. All we want is the machine gun. I'm a gun manufacturer. I'll have a machine gun on the market within three months. A simple trade. One pretty Elizabeth Merchant unharmed, untouched, and in good condition, for one machine gun in equally good condition."

"Bastard," Canyon roared.

Hirum, leading the packhorse, rode up beside Canyon. He obviously had heard the whole thing. There were tears in his eyes. "I don't see what else I can do," Hirum said. "I remember this Smith now, he's a low-down bastard. Steals gun designs like a blood-sucking leech. He has no ethics or morals. He's capable of doing bad things to Elizabeth until I give him the gun."

"Stall him for an hour. I should be able to slip up on them in an hour and free Elizabeth."

"Now you're the one not thinking straight. The minute you leave me, they will sweep in here and grab me and the gun. We have to stick together. They have the winning hand."

"Listen to Hirum Merchant," the booming voice from the brush advised. "He knows just how good we are. We won't hesitate to hurt the girl. Of course, before we disposed of her entirely there would be some liberties taken, such a pretty girl—"

"Bastards," Canyon bellowed. He pulled his six-gun and started to shoot toward the voice, then realized he couldn't. Elizabeth was over there somewhere.

Canyon tried to think of an alternate plan. Nothing jelled. He knew he was looking at the problem emotionally. The best plan would be to sacrifice the girl and save the gun and Mr. Merchant. But he couldn't do that, and even if he tried, Hirum would stop him.

"Look," Hirum said, "all we can agree to do is trade the gun for Elizabeth. Then, as soon as we get her back, we'll try to recapture the gun. That's the best plan I can come up with." He had been speaking in hushed tones so Smith in the brush couldn't hear.

"What do you think?" Canyon asked. "Just so we

save Elizabeth. She means more to me than any old piece of iron."

"But this piece of iron will be tremendously important to the United States Army. Let's try it." Canyon turned his horse to face the brush where he thought Smith was.

"You win, Smith. We'll hand over the gun and trade it for the girl. But not in here. It has to be out in the open by the stream. We'll both come out of the brush at the same time, a hundred yards apart."

"No good, Canyon. I've seen you use a rifle before. You'd try to pick us off."

"Not a chance, Smith. You'll have a hostage. I won't dare shoot, might hit Elizabeth. We make the trade and both can fade back into the brush. I'll give you my word I won't fire at you while we're making the trade. Hell, you'll get the gun, that's what you want."

There was a moment of silence, then Smith called out again. "You've got a deal, Canyon. You two move north fifty yards, and when you see us come out of the brush, you come out. Then Hirum can lead the horse toward us and I'll lead the girl's horse up halfway. We trade there."

"Fine," Canyon called. "We're moving.

"I don't like it," Hirum said. He pulled on the lead line for the packhorse as they started north through the light brush. "He's lying to us. Once I get there with the gun, he can shoot me and keep the gun and Elizabeth both."

"I'm worrying about that. He has us over a barrel. Nothing else we can do right now. If anything goes wrong, I'll get that gun and Elizabeth back if I have to follow them all the way to New York."

Hirum looked up, his eyes sad. "I just wish the army had answered my letter eight months ago. Then nobody knew about my gun and I could have finished it at some army fort and not put Elizabeth in any danger."

"It's an imperfect world, Hirum. We've got to try to

make up for that, any way we can. Remember, if they don't give up Elizabeth, I promise that I'll do everything I can to get her back safe and sound."

They stopped at what they decided was fifty yards, and Canyon rode toward the edge of the brush and looked south. He had picked up a hat at the last place they stayed, and he let it shield his eyes as he watched downstream.

He saw a horse's head appear and he edged out more. He had the Spencer out of the scabbard, with a round in the chamber, and he let it hang behind his mount and out of sight.

"Where's the girl?" Canyon bellowed.

The other man came into sight now. "Where's the gun?"

Canyon motioned for Hirum to lead the packhorse into the open. As Hirum came forward, Canyon saw Elizabeth ride out of the brush on her small roan. She wasn't tied. He couldn't see her expression.

"Come forward," Canyon called.

The other rider and Elizabeth moved along the side of the riverbank in the open, and Hirum and the packhorse moved slowly toward them.

They were still forty yards from Canyon when they met. The man on the horse beside Elizabeth now lifted a six-gun and pointed it at Elizabeth. He said something Canyon couldn't hear, then the four horses and the three riders rode hard back the way Elizabeth had come.

Canyon lifted the Spencer, but he had no target. Smith had made sure he was in front of the other horses and he rode them into the brush quickly and out of sight.

"God damn you, Smith," Canyon bellowed. "You just signed your death certificate!" He pushed his horse back into the brush and worked through to the far side. He rode just out of the trees so he could see south. He expected the party to come out of the trees on this side and ride to the south.

It didn't happen. He moved into the open and raced down the side of the brush. Then he stopped and listened.

Nothing.

He went through the brush again to the bank of the stream and saw many tracks heading south. They had waited until he moved, then they went the other way. He galloped south now, following the tracks. They were running, making good time. But where could they go? They knew he would track them. They would use the two Merchants as protection so he wouldn't simply send a barrage of hot lead at them.

Canyon rode slower now, watching the tracks. Soon they went into the water, but he continued straight across the hock-deep creek and out the other side and back to the main road. There he found marks of a wagon. From what he could tell, the horses had come up to the wagon and then been run off. Their tracks were much shallower as they left, indicating that the passengers and the gun were now on the wagon.

The tracks moved to the north. Perhaps the Smith and Barnes team were also working toward the railroad and a fast trip to the east and their gun-making plant. Perhaps.

Canyon rode hard forward for a half-hour and in the distance he saw the wagon moving along. It was a light wagon designed for a speedy small load and had two horses pulling it. Four other riders were around the wagon.

Canyon left the road and rode at right angles to it for a half-mile, then straight ahead at a gallop until he knew he was past the wagon. He slanted back to the road and spotted the vehicle a half-mile behind. It still had the four guards around it.

He put his horse in a low place out of sight of the road and crawled to some low brush twenty yards from the road. He saw a hill ahead but didn't know how high it might be. He had to settle things right here.

He took out one spare tube of rounds but didn't think he'd have a chance for more than eight shots. First he had to make sure that Hirum was not riding one of the four screening horses. Smith might use him as a shield. Canyon would know soon.

The wagon rolled along at a good pace and the horses kept up with it. The riders kept looking behind them and paid no attention to the front. Canyon knew that he would have to make his shots count. His first shot would give away his position with a pall of smoke. Then he would shoot as quickly as he could. Effective shots.

He had thought of shooting the horses pulling the rig, but decided that they could use it to help get away after he drove off Smith's remaining people. Yes.

The rig came closer. Now he could see three people sitting in the wagon box with its low sides. One was Elizabeth. The other was Hirum, he was sure, so the third one must be Smith.

There were things he should know. Had Elizabeth fired her own pistol in the woods, or had those been warning shots to stop her? Did she still have the deadly little six-shot weapon in her skirt pocket?

Time for him to speculate had ended. The rig was fifty yards away. He decided to target the first rider, and he would shoot to kill. He brought up the Spencer and tracked the man for a dozen yards, then, when he was forty yards away, he centered the sights on the man's chest and fired.

At once he whipped down the trigger-guard lever, bringing in a fresh round. He moved his sights to the second man, who had reacted and looked at the blue smoke about the time Canyon fired the second round.

Canyon checked and saw that two men were blown off their horses. The other two screening guards spurred in the opposite direction. Canyon sent two more shots at the two deserters, then looked back at the wagon. Smith sat there calmly. He had stopped the horses and put the muzzle of his pistol against Elizabeth's head.

"Very nice, Canyon. Good work. I could have used you on my team. You killed my partner, but I still hold the best hand. You want me to kill the little lady, go ahead and shoot again. You do and she and the old man are both dead.

"Sure, you'll get me, but the machine-gun project will be shattered and over. Now, I'll tell you what I'm going to do. I'm going to put my horses in motion and drive out of here. You try anything, anything at all, and this lady gets a bloody hole through her pretty head. You hear me, Canyon?"

"I hear you, bastard."

"Come now, we can be civil. You tried, but you lost. Better luck next time. You try anything and this lady is dead as those two men of mine out there." He picked up the reins, slapped them on the backs of the two horses, and the wagon rolled ahead.

Canyon was figuring his chances on a head shot on Smith, but even then his dying finger could pull the trigger and Elizabeth would be dead. He knew he couldn't let that happen.

Then he smiled. It was just a little after noon. In six or seven hours it would be dark. A lot of things could go wrong in the dark. Smith would never know when Canyon might attack him. He'd have to stay awake every moment. When he finally dropped off to sleep, Canyon would fire and the game would be over.

Four hours later, Canyon still followed the wagon. He was about two hundred yards behind it, making no secret of his position. He was trying to worry Smith half to death. Once it got dark, Canyon would move in close and figure out exactly how to take the man down and get the gun and Hirum and Elizabeth back.

For a moment he lifted his brows. He had thought about getting the gun back first. Interesting.

When dusk came about seven-thirty that evening, Smith had pulled the wagon off at a creek two miles past a small town and tied up both his hostages. He made sure the horses were well watered and then picketed, but he left them harnessed to the wagon.

Smith did not make a fire. He was at least that smart, Canyon decided grudgingly. Without a fire the advantage would be with Smith.

When it was fully dark, Canyon worked his way closer to the camp. There was a moon out but little light came through the maple and linden trees near the creek. The chattering of the stream offered some noise cover for Canyon as he moved forward.

Just inside the shelter of the last group of trees, his eyes adjusted to the darkness and he could make out the lumps around the clearing. One was sitting up against a tree.

Canyon found a rock and he threw it to the far side behind the figure at the tree. There was no movement of the blanket-covered lump at the tree.

A fake, a dummy. So where was Smith? He threw another rock about in the same area, and a six-gun snarled, a flash of light as the weapon's force expended part of the power and some of the light around the cylinder.

The gunman was across from where the forms slept. No, they would be gagged so they couldn't help him. Figured. Canyon knew now where the kidnapper was. Six shots into the area might help. No, Smith had moved by now, rolled silently to a new position. He would have protection, a log or rocks, to absorb any shots. He was good at this. Better than Canyon expected.

Canyon found two more rocks. He threw them both one after the other into the spot where he guessed Smith had rolled to. The man was probably right-handed, so he would roll to his right. The rocks hit with little sound, but Canyon thought he heard a short gasp and a groan, but that was all.

The United States agent checked the area carefully. The kidnapper was far enough out of the line of fire so it would not endanger the hostages. He found a big maple and worked behind its trunk. Then lifted his six-gun and threw two rocks, but there was no response.

"Don't worry Smith, I'm still here. You won't get any sleep tonight."

Canyon shouted the words quickly and pushed behind the tree trunk. His words brought a reaction. Smith must have pushed up on his knees and fired three shots at the sound. The first was four feet wide of the tree and Canyon edged around the trunk and saw where the flash came from.

He lifted his own six-gun and fired four times. When the echoes faded away, he heard nothing but the stream.

Canyon thought of disabling the horses or pulling a wheel off the wagon. He could do either easily. No. He wanted Smith on the road tomorrow. Canyon knew he would have more chances to surprise the man and capture him on the road than holed up here in his little fortress. The road would be better.

What surprise could he have for Smith with daylight? No ideas came at once. He would work on it. Then he had a thought for right now. He took the leather pouch of black powder off his belt and poured half of it out onto the ground beside him, maybe a half-cup. He spread a thin stream of powder back three feet from the pile of explosive and touched it to be sure it was thick enough to carry the fire.

Then he moved back to the start of the powder trail and took out a sulfur match. He struck the match, lay it on the powder train, and watched it start to sparkle and burn. Then Canyon dived six feet away and rolled behind a tree trunk. The powder train led the fire the three feet to the half-cup pile of powder, which went off with a surprisingly large explosion.

"What the hell?" a voice said into the night.

Canyon grinned and settled down behind his tree. He'd catch a nap and be up well before daylight. After many nights of practice he had at last worked out the secret. As he drifted off to sleep, he wondered what he could do to surprise Smith in the morning enough to capture him or at least shoot him dead. There had to be something. He'd let his subconscious work on it and tell him the project first thing in the morning. It had to be something special.

13

Canyon awoke about four A.M. and looked around. Pitch-black, but he realized he'd be in plain sight, come daylight. He studied the dark patch of woods and figured where the wagon must be, then he pulled back thirty more yards to a big black oak he could hide behind and still see out.

There might be a chance to blow Smith out of his boots with the Spencer when he went to the wagon. Then Smith would have to put down his gun and couldn't hold it on Elizabeth.

Maybe. What else?

Nothing else came to mind. He would have to play it as it went, find an advantage along the way. Maybe at the first good-sized town, he could ride right up to the wagon and drag Smith off the driver's seat.

Canyon thought of Elizabeth in that bastard's hands and he growled. He knew he shouldn't become so emotionally involved in his cases, but this small blond lady was not the usual type of person he helped. She was special.

He watched the first hints of dawn, then the false dawn, and at last streaks of light eating up the darkness. As the light grew stronger, he spotted the wagon. Damn! The horses were still hitched. Smith had not let them out of the harness during the night. Figured.

Canyon could see part of one blanket roll through the light brush. They would be moving soon. For a moment he wondered if Smith had sneaked the pair out of the small camp during the night, walking them to the nearest town or farm where he could buy horses. No. Smith would never leave the machine gun. They were there.

Confirmation came five minutes later when Canyon saw a man get up and move around behind cover, rousing the other two from blankets. O'Grady almost had a shot at Smith once, but some light brush probably would have deflected the bullet off the target.

He waited.

Again they made no fire. He didn't know if they had any food or utensils for cooking. No use watching the camp. The horses were the important part now. The rig, the gun. Canyon moved silently through the thick brush until he could see the horses standing patiently in harness waiting to move the light wagon.

He saw Elizabeth helped into the three-foot-high wagon box by her father, who then jumped up and sat beside her.

Canyon checked the Spencer carbine and brought it up to bear on the driver's seat, which was perched on metal staves attached to the sides. There was no conflicting brush here to ruin his shot. A voice sounded over the distance, then Smith came from behind some trees and jumped onto the high seat. He reached for the reins and Canyon fired.

Smith had just raised his arms to slap the reins down on the horses as the shot hit him. The bullet, aimed for his torso, hit his right arm instead, and he fell off the seat into the wagon. The horses took the slap of the falling reins and pulled out of the brush, then turned the easiest way onto the roadway ten yards away and moved north. The reins hung slack over the driver's seat.

"Damned bushwacker," Smith bellowed from the wagon. He was under the low wooden side and Canyon couldn't see him.

"My gun is on the girl again," Smith called. "You back off or both of them are dead. Yeah, you hit me in the arm, but I can still shoot. Back away, Canyon, or else.''

Stalemate. Again. He had to ease back. He'd had one chance to kill the man and save the machine gun and two lives. Now he didn't know what might happen.

The lawman in the next town north . . . Canyon let the idea simmer. Yes, he would ride there, show his credentials, and ask the lawman to take Smith into custody for kidnapping. Yes. He let the wagon pull away to the north, then filtered through the woods to where he left his bay. This morning his chest hurt more than it had last night.

O'Grady brayed in pain as he lifted into the saddle. Damm! Now was no time to have a bullet taken out of him. He circled around the north road and saw the wagon in the distance. He kept riding and just before noon came into a fair-sized town. It would have a sheriff or a deputy or a town marshal. He found the sign that said, ANDOVER CITY OFFICE AND JAIL. The jail was in front.

Canyon eased down off his horse, feeling the clutch of pain through his chest high up.

When he pushed through the door marked CITY JAIL, he found a middle-aged man sipping coffee at a battered desk. There was a gun rack on the wall with three shotguns and a rifle in it. Wanted posters had been tacked to the wall.

The man looked up and nodded. ''Morning, friend.''

''Morning. You the town marshal or sheriff?''

''Town marshal. What's your need?''

Canyon took his leather wallet from an inside pocket and pulled out a letter, which he unfolded carefully. It was his certificate of appointment as a United States agent and signed on White House stationery by President Buchanan. He gave the letter to the lawman and waited while he read it.

"So. The president himself, eh? I never heard of such a lawman as this, but looks like you're for positive. You must need some help?"

"That I do. Canyon O'Grady is my name."

"Marshal Wilson."

They shook hands.

Canyon quickly explained the problem of the kidnapping. "The wagon should be coming through town in a half-hour or so. I need you to stop them. Disarm the man and let me take over the wagon and rescue the two kidnap victims. The United States government will be owing you a letter of thanks."

"Well, I dunno. Not exactly in my jurisdiction."

"Of course it is. If the wagon is in town, it's your responsibility. And your local felony laws must have one against kidnapping. These two people are being held captive at gunpoint."

"Will the president himself send me a letter?" Wilson asked.

"Absolutely."

"Damn. Let's go see what we can do." He reached into the gun case and pulled out two Greener shotguns and tossed one to Canyon.

"Got two rounds in it. We shouldn't need more than that."

They rode to the edge of town on the south and waited.

By two that afternoon, Canyon handed the shotgun back to Marshal Wilson.

"He outsmarted me. Must have thought about me getting some help. He went around town. Is there a road north on either side of town here?"

"Yep. One on each side a mile over. Lots of mile-marker roads around here. Checkerboard in some places."

Canyon thanked him, turned right, and pounded down the mile to the crossroad and checked the dirt roadway. He found tracks of two wagons. One was the same as the wagon he had been following, with narrower steel bands around the wheels.

It was moving north because the wheel tracks covered up part of the two horses' hoof prints. He would be at least an hour behind the rig. Canyon spurred the bay into a gallop for a half-mile, then eased up to a trot and let her cool down for a quarter of a mile at a walk. He could see no wagon ahead on the flatland. The wagon kept on the side road for another two miles, then swung back west toward the main road. He hoped he had the right set of prints. If he didn't, it would be too late to try again.

The land changed as he came to some small sharp hills. Now the same tracks he had followed swung back on the main road and continued north. Ahead he saw something in the roadway. He paused when he came to it and looked down: a white handkerchief.

Canyon got off and picked it up. In the corner was the letter "E" embroidered delicately. It could be Elizabeth's. He had seen her with two white handkerchiefs.

Back on his horse, Canyon rode hard for another mile as the road worked upward sharply again. He urged his mount forward. He saw bits of lather showing up on the bay. He was working her too hard. In another two miles he would have to walk her or he'd be walking himself with a dead horse.

He topped the hill, and below, just starting up another hill ahead, he saw the wagon. Clearly he could make out the two in the back and the gun and the packhorse gear. A man rode the driver's seat. Now he had a bandage around his arm.

Less than half a mile away! The horses would be at a slow walk up the hill. He kicked his bay in the flanks and rode her down the hill. He rode too fast, but he had to. It was now or never. He had to save them, save the gun.

As he rode, he realized this time he thought of saving Elizabeth and her father first.

He was down the hill, the wagon was fifty yards ahead going up. No one on the wagon had seen him yet. As he watched, he saw Elizabeth lift both hands pointing at the driver. He didn't know what she was doing until he heard the report of the handgun. It fired once, then twice, then three times. One of the horses screamed in anger and pain and the team lunged ahead, running fast up the hill.

The driver bellowed something and then a fourth bullet evidently hit the driver.

Smith had turned, his left hand holding a pistol, when the slug hit him in the shoulder and spun him sideways off the high seat and dumped him off the side of the wagon. The team heard the other shot now and both panicked.

A runaway, Canyon realized. The horses were so frightened nothing could stop them. The reins now dragged across their backs, another unusual feeling that spooked them even more.

He could see Elizabeth and her father bouncing around in the wagon. He seemed to be trying to hold down the machine gun.

Then the rig came to the top of the hill and ran along a cliff. The horses were staying on the road, but there was no reason to think they might not veer off at any time. The slightest little change could send them into a new panic.

Canyon whipped the bay with the end of his reins, then slapped her on the flank to urge more speed. Foam flew from her mouth; he could feel her sweat staining through his pants and wetting his legs. He was less than thirty yards behind them now on the flat top of the mesa area.

The horses galloped as fast as they could, eyes wild, nostrils flaring in their total panic. All domesticated training forgotten, only the basic surge of survival touched their small brains.

The trail made a sharp turn ahead to work down the far side of the small plateau.

"Jump," Canyon bellowed.

Ahead he saw Hirum Merchant evidently urging Elizabeth to do just that. He moved her to the back of the rig, but she froze and held on to the tailgate; she couldn't move. Hirum looked ahead at the drop-off, then back at his daughter.

Slowly he pulled her hands from the edge of the wagon. Canyon could see that the horses had not taken the turn; they were galloping full-speed at the edge of the cliff.

"Jump, both of you, jump," Canyon screamed.

At last Hirum got Elizabeth's hands free. He held her over the tailgate of the rig, then tossed her out. He turned and looked at the edge of the cliff and tried to jump himself. But it was too late.

Already the horses had gone over the side, the front wheels of the rig crumbled over ancient rocks and then dropped away.

Canyon pulled up where Elizabeth had fallen and rolled over and over in the dust and dirt. He saw the wagon tilt and then the dazed, frightened face of Hirum Merchant looking over the tailgate.

Then it was all gone—horses, wagon, and Hirum. Canyon rode to the edge of the drop-off. It was higher than he had expected. More than a hundred feet of a sheer rock face fell away to a rocky ledge and then another fifty feet to the bottom of the deep canyon far below.

He rode back to the girl and stepped off the panting bay. Elizabeth had sat up in the dirt. He knelt beside her. A scratch on her forehead brought a red line of blood that soon ran down her skin. She had a bruise on her cheek and she held her right hand tenderly.

"Pa?" she asked. "Where's Pa?"

"I'm not sure, Elizabeth."

"Did you see him save me? He told me to jump and I couldn't. I was afraid, and he picked me up and threw me off. He had plenty of time to get off before then. Where's my daddy?"

She began to cry then and he held her as the tears washed out some of the pain. She looked up at him at last and brushed away the tears. "He went over the cliff, didn't he?"

Canyon nodded.

"We better figure out how to get down there and find him, he probably needs us," Elizabeth said calmly.

It took them an hour to ride double on his horse on the wagon road down the far side of the cliff and then get off the road and work into the gorge itself. Some early river had carved a deep canyon here maybe a million years ago. Then upheavals of land had changed the watercourse and it remained a dry jagged scar.

They left the horse and walked into the lower part of the cut. Canyon found the machine gun's tripod first. It was still folded and seemed little damaged. He offered a silent prayer and they pushed ahead to the spot where they could see the remains of the wagon and the two horses.

Both mounts were dead. Canyon was sure. Neither moved as they came toward them.

"Where's my daddy?" Elizabeth asked. Her face began to break apart. All of her strength had drained away from her. She pushed against Canyon for a moment and cried again. "He can't be alive, can he, Canyon? Nobody could live falling that far, could they? I know that. I just don't want to believe it."

Canyon watched her a moment, then sat down on a big rock and brushed her long blond hair back. He kissed her cheek. "There's a chance he's still alive—yes, a good chance. You stay right here and I'll find him. Promise me you'll stay here?"

She looked up, tears coming again, but she nodded.

Canyon worked forward slowly, watching both sides along the face of the bluff. He found a piece of metal a moment later. It was a part of the machine gun. He frowned. The black metal could have been part of the receiver.

Ten yards farther he found more pieces of metal, all black, all part of the fast gun. The weapon might never fire again. Just ahead he found the barrel. Twenty-six inches long, black, bored for .45 ammunition. It was bent and had been torn free from where it screwed into the gun. Canyon sighed and picked up the barrel, then dropped it. The gun was gone.

He worked faster then, and another twenty yards ahead he saw a human hand trailing past a large boulder. Canyon shook his head as he walked around the rock.

Hirum Merchant lay on a jumble of ragged stones where he had fallen. He had hit and bounced off the rocks to get to this spot. Both legs were broken and twisted unnaturally under him. White bones protruded through his right forearm. Only his face seemed undamaged. The back of his head on the rock was mashed and left a bloody pool under it.

Canyon sat down beside Hirum's body. Slowly he realized what this meant. The inventor was dead. The gun was around somewhere, but probably in three hundred pieces. If he could find all of the pieces, it would still be impossible for him or anyone else to put it all back together again.

The gun was gone, the inventor was dead.

Drawings! The German had made drawings of the mechanism. How many did he get made? Hirum had grabbed them and put them in his shirt when they left the house. Did he still have them?

Canyon felt Hirum's shirt, then opened the buttons, but all he found was a mass of bloody tissue where his chest had been crushed at one point in the fall.

No drawings.

The full impact of it hadn't quite come through to Canyon O'Grady yet. He picked up Hirum and slowly carried him back to where he had left Elizabeth.

She looked up, saw him, and ran up to him.

"I'm sorry, Elizabeth," he said.

She nodded. "I knew it had to be. He gave up his own life to save mine. It'll take me a long time to understand why something like this can happen. He was a good man, a great man. I'll have to live with this for a long time."

Canyon suggested they take Hirum back near the road, then ride into the nearest town. Elizabeth wouldn't permit that. She wouldn't leave him alone out here. At last they lay his broken body over the saddle of the bay and walked along the wagon road to the next small town, Beldon.

They took Hirum to the undertaker. The funeral would be the next day. Canyon registered Elizabeth at the Missouri Hotel and told her he had to go back to the wreck and see if he could find the pieces of the gun.

She nodded and lay down, her hand over her eyes.

Canyon rented a horse from the livery, giving his bay a much-needed rest.

The wreck was five miles from town. He thought it was farther. It was a slow process. He guessed that the gun must have fallen out of the wagon early and hit one of the high rocks and broken apart; then the pieces fell, hitting the rocks at the base of the cliff, shattering the metal pieces again.

He found more of the receiver, of the black part where the automatic mechanics went to make the gun work. He even found the trigger and more of the mechanism. Slowly he went over the rocky area again inch by inch, searching for more of the metal parts.

When he was sure he had most of the gun, he put the pieces in a gunnysack he had brought with him, and walked to his horse. It was dark by the time he got back to Beldon. There was no answer when he knocked on Elizabeth's door. He tried the handle and found it unlocked.

Inside the room was dark.

"Elizabeth?"

There was no answer. He scratched a match and held it up.

Elizabeth lay on the bed. She roused and shielded her eyes from the light. "I'm all right, Canyon."

He lit another match and fired up the coal-oil lamp on the dresser.

"My daddy died today. Hirum Merchant is dead." She looked up at him, then went to the window and stared down on the dark street with splashes of light from the saloons.

"Your father was a brave man. He gave up his life to save yours."

"It was my fault he died," Elizabeth said in a monotone. The fire and drive and vigor were gone from her. "If I hadn't shot the horse, the team wouldn't have run away."

"You had no way of knowing. Don't think about the 'if' things. That won't help. You did what you thought was best at the time."

"My daddy died because of what I did. I'll never forgive myself. Never."

"I think it's time you had some sleep. The funeral will be tomorrow. It's all arranged. In the morning we'll find you a nice black dress at the general store."

"I don't want a black dress. I want my daddy back."

She held out her arms then, and he went to the bed and sat beside her and held her. Elizabeth began to cry quietly against his chest.

It took her fifteen minutes to get her crying done. Then she wiped her eyes and took off her blouse and the long divided skirt and stretched out on the bed.

"I want you to stay with me tonight, Canyon. Not

158

to make love, just to be here and hold me. I need you near me, with your arms around me. Can you do that, Canyon?"

"Yes, of course."

He took off his boots and his shirt and lay down beside her. She came into his arms and sobbed for a few minutes, then she was sleeping. He didn't want to move.

At last he slipped her back on her side of the bed and she didn't wake up. It took Canyon a long time before he could get to sleep that night.

Elizabeth would be all right in a few weeks. That was good.

Hirum Merchant, a genius with arms, had been lost to the world forever.

The Merchant machine gun had died with him. Canyon would take the gunnysack full of parts and pieces to the gunsmiths at Fort Leavenworth, but he had no hope that they could make the Merchant machine gun whole again. He doubted if the gunsmiths there would be able to figure out enough even to learn the principle of the weapon. The drawings were also gone.

The only positive note was that the Germans and the English had not stolen the gun and taken it to Europe. Canyon set his jaw. He knew his boss at the White House and the army brass were not going to be happy with the outcome. He gave a long, tired sigh. He'd fight with the army generals when he got to the fort, but that wouldn't be for two days yet.

14

The next morning, Canyon did buy Elizabeth a black dress and hat and black shoes for the funeral. He hired a buggy and they drove to the cemetery, where the local Congregational preacher gave a short graveside service for this man he had never met. It turned out to be neat and proper and somehow sterile and ridiculous when Canyon thought it through.

On the way back from the cemetery, a half-mile out of town, Canyon could no longer hold down the pain in his chest. It came at him in concentric waves, each one building where the last one stopped until he sagged to one side and then leaned against Elizabeth, looked up at her, and mumbled something; then he lost consciousness.

She took the reins and drove directly to the doctor's office she had seen a block from the hotel.

Two hours later Canyon believed that he was swimming in a gooey mass of molasses and chicken giblet gravy. He was having trouble staying on top of it and he thrashed his arms until they were hopelessly entangled and he couldn't move them. Slowly the sun came through the murk and he kept blinking his eyes, and when they came fully open, he saw only stark whiteness.

He was in a room. He turned his head and saw a large man in a white apron holding down his arms. A few feet behind the man he could see Elizabeth in her black dress and hat. She looked worried.

"Well, now, see, miss. This one ain't dead after all. But it was a good thing you got him here when you did. How long ago did you say he was shot?"

"Three days ago," Canyon said. But the words came out garbled and sounding more like a wheeze and a cough.

"Don't try to talk, young man," the older man said. He let go of Canyon's arms and stared down at him. "You gave us quite a turn, Mr. O'Grady. Your Irish luck pulled you through, I'd say. Had a hell of a time digging out that bullet. Begging your pardon, miss, but it was a job. Didn't go in so far. Some low-powered round, I'd guess. But it broke a rib and then lodged behind.

"Took some digging around. Land sakes, first bullet I pull out of a body in four or five years." He motioned to Elizabeth. "This pretty girl say's she's your friend. Yes, we found your money belt when we operated, and every dollar is there. That pretty girl has it. I'm sorry about her father. Now, you stay put. You're not leaving that bed for at least two days. Then you'll need a buggy to get up to Kansas City. Hear tell that's where you're going."

The doctor tapped Canyon on the forehead. "Hear now, son. You stay right put for at least two days. This is a kind of hospital, just a house next to my office, but I rent it and there's a room for the young lady to use. No argument. I've got some other patients."

He turned and left the room.

Elizabeth came over and sat on a chair beside Canyon. He wasn't sure what the expression on her pretty face meant.

"You had me worried sick, Canyon," she said softly. "I finally decided not to let you die. I'll even be your keeper all the way to Fort Leavenworth. Then you'll be on your own."

"But don't . . ." He tried to talk, but the words didn't come out right.

161

"The doctor said you might talk funny for a while. But you should be chattering away as usual in a day or two." She pushed a pad of paper and a wood pencil to him.

Canyon lifted the pencil and wrote on the pad. "Might be able to put the gun together. If so, you'll own it. Patents, sales to army, etc."

He pushed the pad to her and she read it.

"No. I want nothing to do with it. I saw what it did to those men and horses. No. If you can make it work, fine. Give it to the army."

"What will you do now?" he wrote.

She started to speak, but the white ceiling began to drop down on him and the light coming in the window changed into red and then enveloped him and he drifted into a troubled sleep.

Two days later the doctor said he was fit to travel. He bought a light buggy and hitched his bay to the single-rig harness and they were ready to go. When Elizabeth came, she was wearing her black dress and hat.

Canyon shook his head. He got to the money belt around his waist and took out a twenty-dollar bill.

"Go buy yourself some decent clothes. Spend all of that. When you come back in some real clothes, then we'll go to Kansas City."

Elizabeth glared at him for a moment, then took the bill and left. When she came back, she wore an attractive blue-and-white print dress, a new sunbonnet, and had a small carpetbag with more clothes inside.

"Thank you," she said softly. She reached in and kissed his cheek and then took the reins and drove toward Kansas City.

It took them three days to get to Fort Leavenworth. He reported in to the commandant's office and was quickly put in the army medical ward, where the army doctors examined him and gave him some additional treatment.

For three days he and three of the army's best gun-smiths worked over the gunnysack of machine-gun parts. Canyon drew a rough picture of what the weapon looked like, but he had not seen the inside of it and had no idea what the recoil principle was or how it worked.

After two more days they reconstructed part of the gun, but plainly the gunsmiths did not have any idea how it worked either.

"That's enough," Canyon said after the fifth day. "Thank you, gentlemen, for your help. Will one of your throw this in the nearest trash barrel? The Merchant machine gun will never be a reality."

Elizabeth had been staying in the visitor's section of the big building, where the married officers lived. Canyon had a set of rooms beside hers. He went directly to her quarters and told her that he had given up on ever reconstructing the gun.

"Good," she said. "God must not have wanted man to have such a weapon just yet. Pa must have been ahead of his time. He was too smart for his own good, so God let him die and his weapon was destroyed at the same time."

Canyon nodded seriously, although he had no such notion. He would let her think what she must.

"I've sent a long telegram to my headquarters, explaining what happened. At least the Germans and the English didn't get the gun. I'll be staying here for a few days more until I hear back from Washington and get my clearance from the army doctors that I'm fit for service again."

"Yes, I thought you might be making some plans for your future. I've been doing a lot of thinking about my future, too. Perhaps I wasn't as responsible as I thought as first for Pa being killed down there. I've decided that I should go back to Chicago. Pa has a sister who lives there. She was never very close to Pa. But I'll tell her what happened and see if I can live with her and her family for a time. I might become a poet. Who knows?

There must be something in life that I'm supposed to do—besides get married and have a family, I mean.''

They were in her rooms and she came and sat beside him on the couch. Her lips brushed his and then came away.

"Mr. O'Grady, I want to thank you for teaching me how to be a woman. I understand a lot of things now that I didn't know about before. They all will stand me in good stead. I was thrilled at your touch, but now I know that I want to look for a man who will hold me and love me and also stay with me and care for me as well. You're not that kind of man, Mr. O'Grady."

She sat closely to him and stared at him with her pale-green eyes.

His hand stroked her long blond hair. She turned and then he kissed her firmly on her lips. She sighed.

"Even if you were well enough, I couldn't possibly let you take any liberties with me. I am a weak woman in a strange city and entirely at your mercy . . ."

Canyon smiled, then frowned slightly. "Oh, Miss Merchant, I certainly wouldn't want to take advantage of a lady like you. That would be the farthest thing from my mind. I did think that a friendly good-bye kiss might be in order, however, between good friends such as we are."

She sat close to him, her thigh now gently touching his. "Well, Mr. O'Grady, since we have been good friends, and since we have been through a lot of danger together, I think it would be appropriate if you did give me a simple and chaste good-bye kiss."

"I think that's a wise decision."

He bent and kissed her waiting lips. They parted and his tongue worked inside her mouth and she pressed against him. Slowly she found his hand and lifted it to her breast. His hand caressed her softly. Gently it worked inside her dress to her bare breasts, and she sighed.

"Miss Merchant," he said, breaking off the kiss, "it

seems to me we could say a more meaningful good-bye if we had more room, perhaps in your bedroom."

"Yes, that does seem reasonable. Are you strong enough to walk that far?"

He was. An hour later they lay in each other's arms.

"I'll never meet another man like you, O'Grady. You are so handsome and so damned good in bed. I'll be comparing every suitor I have in Chicago with you. I've decided to put off leaving for a day or two. We can continue our good-byes for a few days until you have to leave. Would that be all right? I'll try not to tire you out too much or interfere with your recuperation."

"Sounds good to me," Canyon said. He tangled his hand in her hair and kissed her cherry lips and relaxed. He liked the way she said good-bye. But already he was wondering just what President Buchanan would have for him to do next. This had not been his most successful mission, but the nation had at least come out even. Somehow he had the idea he might be moving farther west on his next mission. Into the Old West of cowboys and Indians and the wide open spaces. At least he could hope.

Canyon quit thinking about that and went back to a more important job: making sure that Elizabeth had a proper good-bye. He'd never said good-bye to anyone before for three days. Tough duty, he thought, damn tough duty!

Historical Note:
In 1884, just over twenty-four years after Hirum Merchant's machine gun was destroyed, another American, Hirum Maxim, invented his practical and historical machine gun. Maxim shifted his allegiance to England, where he built his Maxim machine guns and was knighted by Queen Victoria. The Maxim machine gun changed the tactics of modern warfare forever.

KEEP A LOOKOUT!

The following is the opening section from the next novel in the action-packed new Signet Western series CANYON O'GRADY.

CANYON O'GRADY #4
SHADOW GUNS

*Missouri, 1859, west of Thousand Hills,
a state half-free and half-slave,
a land where hate was only a
stepping stone to power. . . .*

"She'll be getting herself killed," the big red-haired man muttered aloud. "And she's too lovely for that," he added, his clear blue eyes looking down at the scene at the foot of the hill. The young woman rode her horse full out as she chased the big bay, the lariat in her hand. She had made two tries to rope the running horse from a half-dozen yards behind, and he'd winced each time. He saw that she was trying again and he sent his own horse downhill while his eyes stayed riveted on the racing bay. The horse ran in a huge circle as the girl pursued. It wasn't a wild horse, not with the smooth, well-groomed condition of its coat. But it was worse than a wild horse, the big man knew, it was a powerful animal crazed with fear or hate, filled with emotions more directed than that of a wild horse.

The big man had almost reached the bottom of the hill when he saw the young woman swirling the lariat as she prepared to throw it again. She'd keep herself alive if she missed again, he muttered inwardly, but saw her send the lariat through the air. This time she didn't miss, the loop settled over the horse's neck, and she immediately pulled her own mount to a halt. She started to yank back on the lariat, and the flame-haired man opened his mouth to shout, but it was too late. His lips pulled back in a grimace as he saw her fly from her saddle head-first and slam into the ground. The lasso flew from her hands as she hit, and the big bay skidded to a halt, then turned and started back toward her, its nostrils flared and ears laid back.

The red-haired man swerved his horse to charge forward, just as the big bay came to a halt and reared up on its hind legs. Shouting at the top of his voice, he raced between the young woman on the ground and the bay's flailing hooves. The angry horse took a step backwards, and his sharp-edged hooves struck into the ground. But, though snorting in anger, he remained still. He'd try again, the big flame-haired man knew, seeing the wild fury in his eyes. A quick glance at the girl saw her pushing herself to her feet, her forehead smudged with dirt. It didn't take away from the fine looks of her, he noted.

"Can you run?" he called out and she nodded. "Get over to that hickory over there," he said.

"Can you get him?" she asked as she started to move toward the tree.

"I'll try, but nobody can do it the way you did," he snapped. He heard the big bay's snort of anger, and turned his attention back to the horse. The bay started to back up, then turned, and the big man yanked his lariat from the lariat strap, twirling it in the air even before he began to chase after the bay. He spurred his own bronze-hued horse into a gallop, caught up to the bay and saw the runaway mount immediately begin to veer away in a wide circle. But the horse and rider stayed with him, and the bay shortened the diameter of the circle. The red-haired man edged his own mount up another few feet, almost against the runaway bay's flank, and flung the lariat in a short, accurate toss that sent the loop descending over the other horse's neck.

But he made no attempt to skid to a halt and pull back on the lariat. Instead, he raced almost alongside the bay, pulling the lariat with slow, steady pressure until the other horse began to slow. He tightened the lariat again, using the power and weight of his own horse to help pull back on the rope. Finally, as the bay completed the circle, he began to slow. He still resisted, tried to shake the rope loose, but the steady pressure on the rope remained and he finally broke into a trot. His captor brought him into a tighter circle, then steered the horse beside a tree where the young woman waited. He wrapped the lariat around a low branch and secured the horse in place before he swung from the saddle.

"That was extraordinary," the young woman said. "I guess I went about it all wrong. I've never had to do that before."

"Let's just say you're not ready to take up the wrangler's life yet," the big, flame-haired man said, smiling. "You can't rope him to a stop from way back where you were. Nobody's strong enough for that."

"So I found out," she said ruefully.

"You have to go with him, slow him down with a steady pressure, or you'll have your arms pulled out of their sockets, or break your neck when you go flying," he said. "And we wouldn't want that," he added as he let his eyes survey the young woman with slow deliberateness. He took in a straight, thin nose, delicately flared, thin, black eyebrows, a slender body with breasts that curved in a lovely, long line under a pale yellow shirt, and he gave voice to the rest of what he saw. "Hair black as a raven's wing, eyes to match and skin white as Egyptian alabaster," he murmured.

The thin, black eyebrows arched and a smile edged her lips. "A poet with a lilt in his voice and a wrangler of rare skill," she said. "An unlikely combination indeed."

"Unlikely and untrue, seeing as I can't own up to either," the big man laughed and saw her take in the red of his hair, the roguish cast of his face and the snapping blue of his eyes.

"You can own up to a name, I presume," she said, cool amusement in her almost black eyes. Amusement and interest, he perceived.

"Indeed. It's Canyon O'Grady at your service," he said with a half bow.

Her smile became a soft laugh. "A most unusual name for a most unusual man, I suspect," she said. "I'm Carla Gannet."

Canyon O'Grady let his gracious smile mask the surprise that flashed through him. He accepted her remark with a shrug and turned to look at the big bay again. He was a splendid piece of horseflesh, with a deep chest, strong rump, and well-placed neck. He was a horse made for powerful running. But his ears were still laid back and the wildness still in his eyes. Carla Gannet brought her tall, slender form alongside Canyon to gaze at the horse.

"He's one of my father's horses, but there's only one man who can handle and ride him. I took him out to try to work with him, a foolish thing on my part. He bolted from the exercise ring, I chased him and you know the rest," Carla Gannet said. "He's a mean horse, real bad-tempered. He hates all people except for Owen."

"I take it Owen's the one man that handles him," Canyon said.

"Yes, Owen Dunstan. He's a family friend and one of my gentlemen callers," Carla said.

"A special one?" Canyon smiled.

"Perhaps. He thinks so," she replied. Canyon stepped closer to the horse and studied the animal for a few minutes in silence. The horse stepped backwards at once, his eyes rolling back in his head and his ears going flat. Yet then he took a step forward, a challenging movement. Canyon stepped back and the horse took another step forward.

"He's been made mean," Canyon said, turning to the young woman. Her thin, black eyebrows lowered as a furrow crossed the smoothness of her alabaster brow.

"How can you say that?" she questioned.

"I've seen enough real mean actors," Canyon said. "They've a different kind of eye, and they're ready to charge and trample you anytime they get the chance. He doesn't have that eye. And I've seen wild horses you can't ever really tame. They have their own special brand of wildness, a kind of raging pride they never lose. You can always see that in them. This horse isn't any of those. He's been handled wrong, made to obey instead of to want to obey."

Carla Gannet's black eyes danced with a combination of amusement and admiration as she studied the big, flame-haired man. "You know your horses, Canyon O'Grady," she said. "But Owen wouldn't like hearing that."

"Too bad for Owen," Canyon grunted coldly.

She smiled as she turned to look at Canyon O'Grady's magnificent palomino, taking in the horse with a practiced eye. "This is the most beautiful palomino I've ever seen," she said. "I imagine he's a very special horse."

"He is," Canyon agreed serenely, and rubbed a hand across the pale-bronze hide and mane.

"What do you call him?" Carla Gannet asked.

"Cormac," Canyon said.

The faint smile touched her lips again. "Another unusual name. I might have expected as much," she said.

"King Cormac was one of the four great legendary Irish kings," Canyon explained.

F.M. PARKER CORRALS THE WILD WEST

☐ **THE FAR BATTLEGROUND** 1847. The Mexican War. They were men of conviction who fought for their country without fear, two soldiers, bound together by more than professional comraderie. Each owed the other his life. But now both men are thrust into a painful confrontation that tests the bounds of their loyalty and trust. . . .   (156757—$3.50)

☐ **COLDIRON** It took a man as hard as cold-forged steel to carve himself a sprawling ranch out of the wilderness. Luke Coldiron's killer instinct lay dormant a long time, but now his kingdom is threatened by a private army of hand-picked murderers, and he has to find out whether the still has what it takes to survive. . . .   (155726—$2.95)

☐ **SHADOW OF THE WOLF** Left for dead by a vicious army deserter and a renegade Indian warrior, Luke Coldiron fought his way back to the world of the living. Now he's coming after his foes . . . ready to ride through the jaws of hell if he can blast them into it. . . .   (155734—$2.95)

☐ **THE HIGHBINDERS.** A brutal gang of outlaws was out for miner's gold, and young Tom Galletin stood alone against the killing crew . . . until he found an ally named Pak Ho. The odds were against them, but with Galletin's flaming Colt .45 and Pak Ho's razor-sharp, double-edged sword it was a mistake to count them out. . . .   (155742—$2.95)

☐ **THE SHANGHAIERS** Young Tom Galletin had learned early to kill to survive in a land where the slow died fast. Luke Coldiron was a frontier legend among men who lived or died by their guns. Together they face the most vicious gang that ever traded human flesh for gold—and it looks like a fight to the death. . . .   (151836—$2.95)

Buy them at your local
bookstore or use coupon
on next page for ordering.

The young woman's smile remained as she peered at the big, red-haired man with amused appraisal. "Who are you, Canyon O'Grady?" she asked.

"A wandered, a searcher, a tinker, a mender of whatever needs mending," Canyon replied. "Runaway horses or runaway hearts."

"And a man quicker with words than answers," she laughed, a velvety laugh.

"Never," he said in mock protest, and his attention turned to the distance where a horse and rider raced toward them.

"Owen," Carla Gannet said, and Canyon watched the rider grow larger, slow to a halt and leap to the ground. He took in a tall man wearing a loose-sleeved, dark shirt open at the neck, carefully combed hair, and a handsome face, but one that wore arrogance in it. He noted good shoulders, a flat figure with narrow-hipped grace. Owen Dunstan's eyes went directly to the young woman as he faced her, a riding crop in his right hand and anger in his face.

"Dammit, Carla, you'd no right taking him out of the stall," he said. "You know I'm the only one who can handle him."

"He is Daddy's horse," Carla returned. "I thought the exercise would do him good. He hasn't been out for two days."

"You'd no right, especially two days before the meet," Owen Dunstan repeated angrily.

"My mistake," Carla said.

Canyon saw that Owen Dunstan ignored him as a king ignores a stableboy, and he watched in silence as the man turned to look at the big bay. "You were very lucky, Carla. I don't know how you managed to get him back," Dunstan said to the young woman.

"I didn't. This man did," Carla said, gesturing to Canyon.

Dunstan turned to look directly at the big red-haired man for the first time, a faint arch of his eyebrows his only acknowledgment. "I see," Owen Dunstan said. "Well, if you come back with me I'll see that you're paid for your trouble."

Canyon saw that the arrogance in the man's face was but a reflection of his character. "Do you work at being grateful or does it just come naturally to you, old boy?" he said.

He watched Owen Dunstan take a moment to absorb the answer, and enjoyed the touch of surprise that came into the man's face. "I don't like your tone," Dunstan snapped.

"That makes us even," Canyon answered.

"People don't talk to me in that tone, mister."

"Then look at this as a refreshing change," Canyon replied. Owen was too arrogant to detect the steel behind the smile. He stepped forward, the riding crop raised in one hand.

"Perhaps you need a lesson in manners."

Canyon eyed the riding crop with almost amused tolerance. "The last man who raised one of those to me has never been able to take a drink without pain since," Canyon said, watching Dunstan's face grow florid. But Dunstan had suddenly taken notice of the danger in the big, red-haired man's eyes and he lowered the riding crop.

"Stop it this minute, Owen," Carla Gannet's voice interrupted. "This man saved me and he saved your horse. You owe him an apology."

Dunstan spun on her. "You apologize to him. This has all been your fault, Carla," he growled. He strode to the horse, untied him and swung onto the animal's back. He rode off at a fast trot, not looking back and pulling the second horse along with him. Canyon saw the young woman turn to him.

"I'm sorry," she said. "Good manners desert him when he's upset."

"And you're good at making excuses for him," Canyon remarked. "He doesn't seem worth it."

"He a product of his background, his lifestyle. That's just the kind of thinking and behavior that goes with it," she said.

"Indeed, only most of us aren't bred into arrogance," Canyon answered.

"Let's forget Owen," she said. "I'm very grateful to you and I'd like to know a lot more about Canyon O'Grady. This is a festive week around these parts. Daddy's having a big party tomorrow night at our place. Please come. I'm sure Daddy will want to thank you for saving his daughter's neck."

"I've no fancy clothes," Canyon demurred.

"Come as you are. You'll be my guest," she said and her hand rested against his arm.

"Now how could I turn down being the guest of the most beautiful woman there?" Canyon laughed.

"Then I'll see you tomorrow night at the house. Ask anybody where it is," she said, and he watched the curve of her breasts sway beautifully as she pulled herself onto her horse. She held her hand out and he took it, pressing the soft smoothness of it against his lips. Her smile held the hint of promise in the soft corners of her mouth. "I'll be looking for you, Canyon O'Grady," she said, putting the horse into a trot. He watched her become a small and distant figure riding across the low hills.

"Carla Gannet," he murmured aloud to himself while a smile touched his lips. A stroke of luck, entirely unexpected, he reflected. And he wouldn't be turning his back on it. The day hadn't been a total loss. He had done a good deed, met a beautiful woman and made an enemy. Life was a thing of balances, and his were about to grow more precarious. But then, that's what had brought him to this state called Missouri. The Indians had named it the place of the people of the big canoes. The white man had made it a place of big hopes and big heartaches, a land that seethed with a thousand fires of the spirit. Maybe he could put one out. Or make another burn more brightly. Time would tell, and Carla Gannet was a lovely place to start.